Lowe Golden &

Great Combination High-Class Trotting Horse Sale

at the arena, Tremont and Chandler Streets - commencing Tuesday, May

2, 1893, and continuing until all stock is disposed of, sale commences daily

at 10:30 a.m.

Lowe Golden &

Great Combination High-Class Trotting Horse Sale
*at the arena, Tremont and Chandler Streets - commencing Tuesday, May 2, 1893,
and continuing until all stock is disposed of, sale commences daily at 10:30 a.m.*

ISBN/EAN: 9783337409173

Printed in Europe, USA, Canada, Australia, Japan

Cover: Foto ©Andreas Hilbeck / pixelio.de

More available books at **www.hansebooks.com**

GOLDEN & LOWE'S

Great Combination High=Class

TROTTING HORSE SALE,

AT THE

ARENA.

TREMONT AND CHANDLER STREETS.

Commencing Tuesday, May 2,
1893, and continuing until all
stock is disposed of.

Sale Commences daily at

10.30 A. M.

Compiled by
ALLEN LOWE,
Room 100,
Boston Globe.

BOSTON.
L. Barta & Co., Printers,
1893.

CONSIGNMENTS.

CONDITIONS OF SALE,

ARENA, BOSTON.

---

(1) The Sale will be conducted in the interest of both buyer and seller.

(2) Stock will be sold in the order catalogued. Each animal will be sold without reserve. No by-bidding will be allowed.

(3) The management acts solely as agent and does not hold itself responsible for any representation, warranty or guarantee, of any kind, verbal or otherwise. The name of the owner is given with each entry, and he alone is responsible for all statements.

(4) In case a warranty of any animal is intended, it will be so stated in the catalogue or by the auctioneer at the time of sale. In absence of such special statement, each animal will be sold as it stands.

(5) Descriptions:

The descriptions printed in the catalogue are received from owners, and are given in order that intending purchasers may form a reasonably correct opinion of the animals before seeing them. Animals described as registered are either recorded in the American Trotting Register or have been accepted for that purpose. The word " Standard " implies only that the animal is qualified for (but not necessarily registered in) the Standard Department of the Register. Beyond the fact that the registered blood lines correspond with the Trotting Register and Thorough-Bred Stud Book, and that reasonable precautions have been taken in the statement of unregistered blood lines, or parts of blood lines, no representations are made regarding them and nothing is guaranteed. Descriptions as to height, age, weight, marks, and speed of horses are approximated by owners and these, with all records, trials, matter of current history, and accredited reports are given in the belief that they are correct, but bidders should examine for themselves, bearing in mind that all such matters depend largely upon estimates of memory and may not be exact.

(6) Bidding:

Each animal will be sold to the highest bidder. When a dispute arises between two or more bidders as to which is the highest, the auctioneer shall decide, and if his decision is doubted, the animal shall be offered again, and unless the party objecting makes a larger bid, the animal will be sold to the party in whose favor the auctioneer originally decided.

(7) **Payments:**

All payments must be made in cash. A deposit of twenty-five per cent. of the price bid must be made in cash immediately upon the sale of each animal, in default of which the auctioneer may at his option declare the sale void, and the animal may be at once resold, any loss to be borne by the first purchaser. The balance of the purchase money must be paid in cash within twenty-four hours from time of sale. If the balance is not paid, or satisfactorily secured within the time limited as aforesaid, the deposit of twenty-five per cent. will be forfeited as an agreed liquidation of damages, and the sale otherwise held void.

(8) **Proof of warranty:**

The purchase price of each animal will be retained by the management for four days from date of sale (unless the purchaser waives this protection by accepting a previous delivery), thus giving an opportunity for the verification of any warranty. Upon proof of a false warranty, the sale will be cancelled and money refunded. At the expiration of four days, if the warranty has not been challenged, or if the animal has been delivered, the management will be at liberty to pay the money to the owner. All warranties must be tested and decided before the animal leaves our possession, as after that no claim will be received or considered. In case of a controversy as to any warranty, the management will appoint some disinterested party to examine the animal, and the decision of the person so appointed shall be final and binding upon all parties. The management, however, assumes no personal responsibility for, and no action shall accrue to either party against the management, because of such decision. The person against whom the decision is made must pay the fees for the examination.

(9) **Delivery:**

No animal will be delivered until it is paid for. No payments will be accepted at the stable. The purchaser must pay his bill (together with all charges for keep) at the office in the Arena Building, Tremont and Chandler Streets. A written order upon the superintendent of the stable will be given for each animal, at the time the bill is paid, and no animal will be delivered except upon the production and surrender of such order. No delivery will be made on an order written by the purchaser. The superintendent is instructed to recognize orders from the office only.

(10) Keeping:

No charge for keeping will be made to the purchaser for any animal removed on the day of sale. But thereafter a charge of $2 a day will be made, to be paid upon delivery of the animal. This rule is rendered necessary from the fact that the stable room is needed for other horses to be sold on succeeding days.

(11) Conditions:

Our charge for services in making a sale is ten per cent. upon the purchase price; no charge however to be less than $30. In case a sale fails through any misrepresentation on the part of the seller, ten per cent. upon the price bid will be charged, together with the expense of keeping. If the animal is passed without a bid, a charge of $30 will be made to the owner for expenses, of advertising, etc., and the same charge will be made for each animal catalogued and subsequently withdrawn. The full commission of ten per cent. will be charged upon the gross amount of the price obtained in all cases where an animal listed is sold privately prior to the sale. A charge of $1 per day will be made for the keep of each animal up to and including day of sale.

(12) Telegraph orders:

Orders by mail or telegraph from responsible parties will be carefully observed, and in case of purchase, the animal will be held subject to Boston or New York draft.

CONSTANTINE, 10870.

The finest type of a trotting stallion yet produced.

Two-year-old trial, 2:26; four-year-old record, 2:19¾ ; five-year-old record, 2:12½.

Sired by

WILKES BOY, 3803.

Four-year-old record, 2:24½.

At twelve years old the sire of more trotters with records better than 2:10 than any other stallion in the world, and is the sire of the only yearling that ever beat 2:30 in a race on a regulation track.

Sire of Constantine, race record, 2:12½ ; St. Vincent, race record, 2:13½ ; Grattan, race record, 2:17¼ ; Angelina, race record, 2:18¼ ; Sternberg, race record, 2:18¾ ; Nellie A. (yearling), race record, 2:20¾; Wilkes Lad (p.), race record, 2:22; Abbadone (p.), race record, 2:24; and ten others with records of 2:30 or better.

Dam, KINCORA . . . . by MAMBRINO PATCHEN, 58.
(Great brood-mare.) The dam of Constantine, 2:12½; J o s i e King, 2:29¼ (the dam of Nelly Aldine, trial, 2:19¼); and Constance, 2:35¼.

Sire of the dams of Ralph Wilkes, 2:13½ ; Guy Wilkes, 2:15¼; Honri, 2:17; Baron Wilkes, 2:18; and 79 others in 2:30.

2d dam, KITTY TRANBY . . . . . by MAMBRINO TRANBY.
(Great brood-mare.) Dam of Glen Wilkes (4), 2:25; Wilkes Girl, trial, 2:35 on half-mile track.

Son of Mambrino Patchen, whose sons have sired the dams of Allerton, 2:09¼; Axtell (3), 2:12; New York Central, 2:13½ ; Mary Marshall, 2:12¾ ; and many other race horses.

3d dam, BETTY BROWN . . . . . by MAMBRINO PATCHEN, 58.
(Great brood-mare.) Dam of Wilkes
Boy, 2:24½; Anglin, 2:27½;
Belle Clay, dam of Amie King,
2:22½; Socratist, 2:25; Macey,
2:26½; Kitty Patchen, the dam
of Georgiana, 2:26¼; Patchen
Wilkes, 2:29½ (sire of Divan
(3, p.), 2:15¼; Lissa (4), 2:17;
Henrico (3), 2:17¾; Favora,
2:19½; etc.); Aileen (dam of
Ellerslie Wilkes, 2:28¾; Lydia
Wilkes, 2:27¾; and St. Vincent, 2:13½); Kitty Tranby
(dam of Glen Wilkes, 2:25;
and of Kincora, dam of Constantine, 2:12⅛).

> The sire of London, 2:20½; Katie
> Middleton, 2:23; and 22 others in
> 2:30; and the progenitor of 645
> trotters with records of 2:30 or
> better.

4th dam, PICKLES . . . . by MAMBRINO CHIEF, 11.
Grandam of Wilkes Boy, 2:24½;
sire of 18 in the 2:30 list at 12
years old.

> Sire of the dams of Red Wilkes, Di-
> rector, 2:17; Onward, 2:25¼, etc.;
> grandsire of the dam of Jay Bird;
> and other sires

5th dam . . . . by BROWN'S BELLFOUNDER.

> Sire of the grandam of Belmont,
> sire of 41 in the 2:30 list; and of
> sons that have sired Belle Vara,
> 2:08¾; Lobasco, 2:10¾; Cheyenne,
> 2:14¼; Junemont, 2:14; Pamlico,
> 2:16¾; Manager (p), 2:09¾; Lock-
> heart, 2:13; Sarcanet, 2:16½, etc.

6th dam . . . . by GREY EAGLE.

> Sire of the grandams of Piedmont,
> 2:17¼; Catchfly, 2:18¼; Paul
> Hacke, 2:24½; Almont Eagle,
> 2:27, etc.

Description.— Constantine is a blood bay horse, with star and hind ankles
white, 15¾ hands high, foaled in 1887, and bred by Mr. Timothy Anglin, Lexington, Ky. In size, color, style, and general conformation he is as near perfection
as it is possible for a horse to be, and in the combined points of superior individuality, high breeding, and extreme speed we believe he stands without an equal.
The George Wilkes-Mambrino Patchen cross, of which Constantine is the fastest
trotting representative by the records, is, without doubt, the most successful and
fashionable cross among trotters. It has produced such performers and race-
horses as Allerton, 2:09¼; Ralph Wilkes, 2:13½; Guy Wilkes, 2:15¼; Baron
Wilkes, 2:18; and many others, while in the stud it has given us such successful
sires of early and extreme speed as Alcyone, Alcantara, Guy Wilkes, Simmons,
Wilkes Boy, Barron Wilkes, etc. Since these stallions have proved and are proving themselves so successful in the stud, we believe that we are justified in pre-
dicting that Constantine, so much more intensely bred in the same bloodlines
and with a faster record, will prove even more successful.

He will make the season of 1893 at $300 the season, money due October 1st,
with a free return privilege, should mare not prove in foal, for the mare bred, or
any other approved mare in her place, until a live foal is obtained, provided the
horse is alive and still owned by us.

DON CARLOS, 2097.

(Standard.)

Record at four years, 2:23¼ ; 2:25; 2:23½ ; present record, 2:23.

Sire of Otis Shaw, 2:19¼ ; Carldon, three-year-old record, 2:25½ ; Carldon, four-year-old record, 2:22¼ ; Alspur, 2:24½ ; Carlos, 2:27; Howdy, record, 2:33, and timed separately in a race in 2:27; Revolver (trial) 2:27; Princess Eboli (trial) 2:27; Topsey (trial) 2:29.

Sire,

CUYLER CLAY, 2796.

Dam, LADY ABDALLAH . . . . by ABDALLAH, 15 (Alex).
  Dam of Don Carlos, 2:23; Gran-   Sire of Goldsmith Maid, 2:14; Rosa-
  ville, 2:26; Halcyon, trial,   lind, 2:21¾ ; Thorndale, 2:21¼
  2:21½ ; Argyle (sire of Lady of   (sire of Edwin Thorne, 2:16¼);
  Lyons, 2:23¾, and Fiction,   Major Edsall, 2:29 (sire of Robert
  2:24¼); Lady Ayres (dam of   McGregor, 2:17½), and St. Elmo,
  Lottie Thorne, 2:27, and Byerly   2:30.
  Abdallah, sire of Jerome
  Turner, 2:15½).

2d dam, AYRES MARE . . . . . . by ——
  A superior trotting mare, breeder
  and pedigree not traced.

Description. — Don Carlos has fully demonstrated his ability to get trotters and race horses. Besides the colts mentioned above a number of others have shown their ability to obtain records of 2:30 or better. Among them is "Richball" whom Mr. John Shepard, of Boston, drove double with Arab 2:15 and could beat 2:30 whenever driven for it. "Wisteria" trotted last year in a race at New London, Conn., in 2:33½ over a poor half mile track. "Red Briar," owned by J. M. Darnaby, Muir, Ky., trotted in 2:42 as a two-year-old, and had she not met with a serious injury, would have beaten 2:30 long ago. "Celia F." trotted in 2:59 to a road cart as a yearling and can beat 2:30 whenever trained, and "Sweetmeat," full sister to Richball, that was knocked off at the Arena Building, last spring, for $150, immediately went out and won the yearling race at Marsh-field, Mass. We might go on and mention others but we think we have said enough to show that Don Carlos' colts trot and trot fast.

For reference only.

IVANEER, 6250.

Brother in blood to Sunol, 2:08¼; and full brother to Veda, 2:26¼.

(Standard.)

Sire,

ELECTIONEER, 125.

Sire of Sunol, 208¼; Norval, 2:14¾; Palo Alto, 208¾; Sweet Rose (1), 2:25¾; Arion (3), 2:10½; Advertiser (3), 2:16; Truman, 2:12; Anteeo, 2:16¼, and 124 others in 2:30.

Dam, ISMA . . . . by GEN. BENTON, 1755.
Dam of Veda, 2:26¼; Ivanhoe (trial, pacing), 2:23, and has trotted quarters 35 and 36 seconds at Palo Alto.

by GEN. BENTON, 1755.
Sire of Daley, 2:15; Sally Benton, 2:17¾ as a four-year-old; Bonnie, 2:25 as a four-year-old, and 15 others better than 2:30, and of the dam of Sunol, 2:08¼; Truman, 2:12, and 21 others in 2:30.

2d dam, IRENE . . . . by MOHAWK CHIEF.
Dam of Ira, 2:24½ and Stanford 2:26½ and g. d. of Veda, 2:26¼.

by MOHAWK CHIEF.
Sire of the dams of Lot Slocum, 2:17¼; Sallie Benton, 2:17¾ as a four-year-old and Eros, 2:29½, and 10 others in 2:30.

3d dam, LAURA KEENE . . . . . by HAMBLETONIAN, 10.
Own sister to the dam of Alban, 2:24: Marion, 2:26¾; Merriment, 2:26½; g. d. of Ira, 2:24½, and Stanford, 2:26¼.

by HAMBLETONIAN, 10.
Sire of Dexter, 2:17¼; Nettie, 2:18, and 38 others.

4th dam, FANNY . . . . by EXTON ECLIPSE.
G. d. of Alban, 2:24; Marion, 2:26¾, and Merriment, 2:26½.

by EXTON ECLIPSE.
Son of American Eclipse, and sire of the grandam of Jay Gould, 2:20½.

5th dam . . . . by SEAGULL.

6th dam, LADY MARVIN . . . . . by YOUNG TRAVELLER.

Description. — We are more than satisfied with Ivaneer as a stock horse, and believe had his colts had the opportunities of many horses' get, that as a sire, he would equal any horse of his age. His colts as yearlings have shown us a phenomenal amount of speed and pure trotting action, but they have all been sold as yearlings in this city (Boston) and we have heard of only one that has been trained. He is out of a strictly running bred mare (by Imp. Glenelg) and his owner, Mr. David H. Blanchard, Boston, Mass., writes us that he showed him a full mile last year as a two-year-old in 2:42½. Another filly by him out of a common work mare, showed us a 2:30 gait before she was half broken, but contracted a skin disease and had to be turned out. She is now in good condition and we expect to put her in the list this year. In fact we never heard of anyone who regretted breeding to this horse or buying one of his colts.

For reference only.

STAMBULA, 11772.

Trial, 2:30½; last half in 1:12.

(Standard.)

Sire,

STAMBOUL.

Record 2:07½.

Sire of Murtha, 2:17; Sweetwater (2), 2:26; Daghestan (2), 2:25½; Nadjy, 2:26; Redondo (4), 2:23; Harry Winchester (3), 2:24¼, and 5 others in 2:30.

Dam, CHOICE . . . . by DICTATOR.
Half-sister to Coralloid, 2:13½;   Sire of Jay Eye See, 2:10 (pacing
sister in blood to Phallas,   2:06¼); Phallas, 2:13¾; Director
2:13¾.   (the sire of Directum (3), 2:11¼;
  Direct, 2:05½; Evangeline (4),
  2:11¼, etc.), and the dam of Nancy
  Hanks, 2:04, etc.

2d dam, CORAL . . . . by CLARK CHIEF.
Dam of Coralloid, 2:13½ and Colon   Sire of Croxie, 2:19¼ and 5 others
(the dam of Semicolon, 2:13¾   in 2:30, and the dams of Martha
and Patchmore, 2:30).   Wilkes, 2:08; Phallas, 2:13¾; Miss
  Majolica, 2:15, etc.

3d dam, CASSIA . . . . by C. M. CLAY, JR., 22.
* Dam of Caliban, 394. Rec. 2:34.   Rec. 2:35¼. Sire of Harry Clay, 2:23¼;
Sire of C. F. Clay, 2:18, and 5   Durango, 2:23¾, and grandsire of
others in 2:30.   32 in 2:30.

4th dam, OLD BECK, s. t. b . . . . by a son of MARK ANTHONY.

5th dam   . by INSTRUCTOR, son of Virginian.

6th dam   by CHESTERVALE HORSE.

7th dam . . . . ROMULUS, son of Bacchus.

Description.—Stambula's oldest colts are coming two years old, and were sold last spring in the Arena Building this city. One of his fillies, out of a mare by Pancoast, which was bought by Mr. John O'Conner, of Bromfield St., Boston, and returned to the farm to be kept and trained, trotted a half mile last fall (as a yearling), in 1:19, last quarter in thirty-seven seconds, and eighth in seventeen seconds (a 2:16 gait). Another filly, bought and returned by the same gentleman, showed us quarters in 45 seconds. Those that remained in the east were equally as promising as these two, and if given a chance are sure to develop plenty of speed.

Consignment of John R. Graham.

No. A.   # REGAL SON.

Bay colt, foaled February 2, 1893.

Bred by John R. Graham.

BY

CONSTANTINE, 10870, 2:12½.

(See front of catalogue.)

Dam, DEL ROSE . . . . by DEL SUR, 1098, 2:24.
    Sister to Don Thomas, 2:20.   Sire of four from 2:10¾; sire of dam
                                   of Lady H., 2:18.

2d dam, VESTUE . . . . by MAMBRINO PATCHEN, 58.
    Dam of one in 2:20.   Sire of 22 trotters; 39 sons with 100;
                                   65 dams of 82, including 18 in
                                   2:20.

3d dam, KATE . . . . by MAMBRINO MESSENGER, 218.
                                   Sire of Lewinski, 2:25¼, etc.

Description. — Here is the prize of the year. It is the first Constantine colt ever bred by Graham & Conley and out of one of the finest mares ever owned at Briar Hill. Race horses of the stripe of this sire are very few, and Del Rose is sister to one of the gamest trotters that ever looked through a bridle. Here is a future champion and is a fair sample of the way Constantine breeds. Don't pass over Regal Son if you want a sure trotter and a future grand young sire. He will be sold with his dam, No. B in this catalogue. He is the image of his sire.

No. B.   # DEL ROSE.

Full sister to Don Thomas, 2:20.

Bay mare, foaled 1882.

Bred by L. J. Rose.

BY

DEL SUR, 1098, 2:24.

Sire of 4 from 2:10¾; sire of the dam of Lady H., 2:18.

Dam, VESTUE . . . . by MAMBRINO PATCHEN, 58.
    Dam of Don Thomas, 2:20.   Sire of 22; 39 sons of 100; 65 dams
                                   of 18 in 2:20, and 82 in 2:30.

2d dam, KATE . . . .   by MAMBRINO MESSENGER, 2:18.
Sire of Lewinski, 2:25¼.

Description.—Del Rose, foaled 1882, is a bay mare, 15½ hands high; bred
by L. J. Rose, Los Angeles, California. She is a splendid mare individually, of
fine size, handsome, and stylish, is by a half-brother to the phenomenal trotting-
sire, Sultan, who has seventeen in the list at thirteen years of age. Then her
dam is by the greatest brood-mare sire of the greatest brood-mare family, and she
has two other Mambrino crosses through both grandams. Del Rose has a fine
turn of speed, and her action is magnificent. At Mr. Rose's sale in Chicago, just
after her arrival from California, as a two-year-old, she trotted a half in 1:17¼,
the last quarter in 0:37. Her son, by Constantine, shows what kind of colts she
produces, and she is booked to Ralph Wilkes, Col. John E. Thayer's grand young
horse, and service can be bought by her purchaser if desired. Regal Son will be
sold with her.

No. C.   HAL ROLFE.

Bay gelding, foaled 1889; bred by Graham & Conley.

BY

BROWN HAL, 16935, 2:12½.

Sire of Storm, 2:08½; 4 in 2:20; 9 in 2:30; dam of Ialene, 2:21¼; son of Tom Hal;
dam, the dam of Little Brown Jug, 2:11¾, etc.

Dam, BELLE ROLFE . . . . . .   by TOM ROLFE, 306, 2:33½.
Sire of Sleepy Tom, 2:12¼; Gem,
2:13¼, and 5 others; 2 speed getters;
2 dams of speed.

2d dam, WOODSTOCK BELLE . . .   by WOODSTOCK, 873.
Sire of Royal John and the dam of
Little Witch.

3d dam, LADY DRACO . . . . .   by FURMAN'S BLACK HAWK.
Dam of Draco Prince, 2:24¼.

Description.—Here is a pacing-bred pacing gelding that is a ready-made
race horse. He can show fast, and prior to the sale can be seen at Col. J. M.
Galvin's stable at Mystic Park. A pacing mare out of Belle Rolfe is to be trained
for George Haddock this year, and can beat 2:20. Graham & Conley sold Allen
Lowe, 2:16½, at their sale last year, and here is another equally fast pacer. Do
not let this fellow slip out of your hands.

Consignment of Graham & Conley.

No. 1.   **RIFLE BALL.**

Sire,

DON CARLOS, 2097.

Record 2:23.

Sire of Otis Shaw, 2:19¼; Carldon (4), 2:22¼; Alspur, 2:24½; Carlos, 2:27.

1st dam, LADY ALMONT . . . . by STAR ALMONT, 6673.
                               Sire of the dams of Bonhomie, 2:17¼; Catherine Leyburn, 2:20; Rose Leyburn, 2:21; and others in 2:30.

2d dam, SARAH McDOWELL . . . by BILLY G. MORGAN.
                               Son of Justin Morgan, sire of Wick, 2:26¼; Lady Lowe, 2:28; and the dam of Saul E., 2:30.

3d dam . . . . by CAPTAIN WALKER.
                               Sire of the dams of Harry Welkes, 2:13½; Charley Friel, 2:15¾; General Garfield, 2:21; and 3 others in 2:30.

4th dam . . . . by TRUMPETER.
5th dam . . . . by MERCER.
6th dam . . . . by CADMUS.

Description.—Chestnut colt, foaled 1892; bred at Briar Hill Farm, Lexington, Ky. Good size, well proportioned, sound, and very good gaited.

Houghton & Dutton,

BOSTON, MASS.

· · · · ·

IMPORTERS AND RETAILERS

OF

DRY AND FANCY GOODS.

English, French and German China, Glass,
> Silverware,
> > Clocks,
> > > Bric a brac, etc.,
> > > > Carpets,
> > > > > Rugs,

Lace Curtains,   Furniture,
> Draperies of all Kinds,
> > Cloaks,
> > > Suits,
> > > > Jewelry,

Ladies' and Gents' Boots and Shoes,   Confectionery,
> Wall Paper,
> > Lamps,
> > > Groceries,
> > > > Musical Goods,
> > > > > Horse Clothing and Bicycles.

JAMES R. HILL & CO.,

34-36 Federal St., 131-133 Congress St.,

BOSTON, - - - MASS.

MAKERS OF

FINE CUSTOM HAND-MADE HARNESS

FOR ALL PURPOSES.

DEALERS IN ALL FURNISHINGS FOR

THE HORSE, THE STABLE, THE CARRIAGE.
TURF GOODS A SPECIALTY.

Manufactory at Concord, N. H. Only Makers of " The Concord Harness."

J. R. HILL & CO.,

34-36 Federal St., Opposite Hancock Building.

No. 2. **JUDGE RENO.**

(Standard.)

Sire,

DON CARLOS, 2097.

Record 2:23.

Sire of Otis Shaw, 2:19¼; Carldon (4), 2:22¼; Alspur, 2:24½; Carlos, 2:27.

Dam, THORNLEAF.
    Standard. Full sister to Thornburg, 2:21½.

Sire, Judge Advocate, 1263; sire of Thornburg 2:21½; Romulus, 2:24¼; Hortense, 2:26½; son of Messenger Duroc; sire of Elaine, 2:20; Prospero, 2:20; Charley Champlin, 2:21¾; Dame Trot, 2:22; John D., 2:23½; Lancelot, 2:23; and 16 others in 2:30.

2d dam, LADY RENO . . . . . . by GENERAL GRANT.
    Dam of Thornburg, 2:21½.

Son of Drew Horse (sire of Dirigo, 2:29; General McClellan, 2:29, and Stella, 2:33).

3d dam, FANTINE . . . . by DREW HORSE, 114.

Sire of the dams of Midnight, 2:18¼, Iron Age, 2:19¼; Volunteer Maid, 2:27; Minnie Moulton, 2:27¼; and Iolanthe, 2:30.

Description.—Chestnut colt, foaled 1892; bred at Briar Hill Farm, Lexington, Ky. Good size, sound, shapely, and good gaited.

J. M. E. MORRILL,

PRIVATE RESIDENCES AND LARGE PUBLIC BUILDINGS.

Also Stables for Stock Farms.

148 CENTRE ST., DORCHESTER. TELEPHONE CONNECTION.

No. 3.   **DEY DUDLEY.**

(Standard.)

Sire,

DON CARLOS, 2097.

Record 2:23.

Sire of Otis Shaw, 2:19¼; Carldon (4), 2:22¼ ; Alspur, 2:24½; Carlos, 2:27.

Dam, IVY.
Standard.   Sister to the dam of
Carlos, 2:27.

Sire, Mambrino Dudley, 967; record, 2:19¾; sire of Crescendo, 2:24; Gretna (4 yrs.), 2:22¼; and three others in 2:30, and the dams of Carlos, 2:27; Alspur, 2:24½.

2d dam, MYRTLE . . . .
Record 2:25½. Sister to Charley B., 2:25 (sire of 18 in the 2:30 list), dam of Myrtlewood, 2:25¼; g. d. of Carlos, 2:27.

by CHAMPION, 807, (King's).
Sire of George B. Daniels, 2:24; Nettie Burlew, 2:24; Golden Girl, 2:25¼; and five others in 2:30.

3d dam OLD JANE . . . .
Dam of Charley B., 2:25 (sire of 18 in the 2:30 list); Myrtle, 2:25½; Maggie, 2:34 to wagon; Oneida Maid, 2:36, and Lady Whitefoot, 2:48 as a four-year-old in 1861.

by NIMROD.
Son of Zeiley's Eclipse, by American Eclipse.

4th dam . . . .
by MESSENGER (Dey's).
Son of Liberty, by Coriander, by Imp. Messenger.

Description.—Chestnut colt, foaled 1892; bred at Briar Hill Farm, Lexington, Ky. Good size, strong, and stoutly made, sound, and very promising gaited.

SHEPARD, NORWELL & CO.

Bargains for Men.

500 Dozens of Short Bosom Shirts (unlaundered),
open back and front.

PRICE 50c. EACH.

ASK FOR THE ORIENT SHIRT.

PERFECT FITTING.

NECK WEAR. 500 DOZENS OF 4-IN-HANDS,

Princess,   Ascot,   Teck,   Puff.

Also Band Bows and Shield Bows, and the
NEW TIE

Graduated Ascot,

the fashion of this season.

This magnificent line of Scarfs all at

50c. each.

Shepard, Norwell & Co., Winter Street and Temple Place.

2:17 AUTOGRAPH. 2:17

The Handsomest, Best, and Fastest Trotting Son of Alcantara.

SIRE OF . . . { SPIERA . . . . 2:24¼.
RAPID TRANSIT . . 2:29¼.

BY

ALCANTARA, 2:23,

Sire of 56 in the 2:30 List,

SON OF

GEORGE WILKES, 2:22	ALMA MATER.
Sire of HARRY WILKES, 2:13½, and 78 others in 2:30 or better.	Dam of 6 in the 2:30 list, including ALCYONE, 2:27, sire of MARTHA WILKES, 2:08, the champion race trotter of the world.

Dam, ... FLAXY,

Dam of AUTOGRAPH, 2:17, WHITEWINGS, 2:24½, BLONDINE, 2:24¾, ETIQUETTE, 2:28½.

DAUGHTER OF

KENTUCKY CLAY,	YOUNG FLAXY,
By Strader's Cassius M. Clay; dam, the Rodes Mare, dam of Lady Thorn, 2:18¼, and Mambrino Patchen.	By Telegraph, son of Vermont Black Hawk.

AUTOGRAPH is a beautiful bay, of good size, very handsome, stylish, and fast. He imparts these qualities to his offspring. He will make the season of 1893 at **MUSTER HILL FARM, New Braintree, Mass.** Terms **$100** cash, with usual return privilege. The pasturage at this farm is unsurpassed by that of any in New England.

DYNAMITE Sire, Midas (sire of the game trotting mare Miss Edith, 2:19), by Onward 2:25¼, out of Cachuca (dam of Catchfly, 2:18¼), by Almont. Dam, Cyclone by Stockbridge Chief, Jr., son of Magic, by American Clay, 34. **Terms, $35.**

MUSTER HILL FARM is reached from West Brookfield on Boston & Albany R. R., and from New Braintree on the Massachusetts Central. Mares met at and shipped from these stations free of charge. Best of care guaranteed while mares remain at farm, but no liability on account of accidents and escapes. For further particulars address **MUSTER HILL FARM, New Braintree, Mass., or GEO. A. LITCHFIELD, 53 State St., Boston, Mass.**

No. 4. TAWNY BELLE.

(Half-sister to Howdy [4], 2:33.)

Sire,

IVANEER, 6250.

Son of Electioneer, 125.

Sire of Sunol, 2:08¼; Palo Alto, 2:08¾; Arion (3), 2:10½; Truman, 2:12; Norval, 2:14¾; Sweet Rose (1), 2:25¾; Advertiser (3), 2:16; Anteeo, 2:16¼; and 124 others in 2:30.

Dam, BROWNIE . . . . Dam of Howdy, yearling record 3:01¼; two-year record 2:39; four-year record 2:33.	by SELIM. Son of Innis' Glencoe (Thor).
2d dam . . . . G. d. of Howdy, 2:33.	by AMERICAN BOY.

Description.—Brown filly, foaled 1892; bred at Briar Hill Stock Farm. Good size, fine shape, sound, and full of nerve and vim, with a good trotting action.

No. 5. MAY SANDERS.

(Standard.)

Sire,

STAMBULA, 11772.

Trial 2:30½; half in 1:12.

Son of Stamboul, 2:07½; sire of Murtha, 2:18; Daghestan (2), 2:25½; Redondo (4), 2:23; Sweetwater (2), 2:26; Nadjy, 2:26; Harry Winchester (3), 2:27¼; and 5 others in 2:30.

SIR WALTER, Jr.,

Winner First Prize for Handsomest Trotting Stallion.

Boston Horse Show, Oct., 1891.   Rich Dark Chestnut, 15-3 hands high.

HAMBLETONIAN, DOUBLE CROSS.

EXTREME SPEED. AMERICAN STAR BLOOD FROM HIS FASTEST TROTTER.

GILT EDGE BREEDING. CLAY BLOOD, DOUBLE CROSS.

Five-year-old
RACE RECORD
2.18 ¼
To the old high wheel.

THOROUGHBRED BLOOD.

From such as imp. Margrave, imp. Tranby, and the great four-mile race horse Wagner.

Williams Farm, Jamaica Plains, Mass., $100 Season, with Usual Return Privilege.

6 MILES FROM BOSTON.

For further particulars address, **WALDO T. PEIRCE,**

Telephone Connection.   ~ 23 BELLEVUE ST., BACK BAY, BOSTON, MASS.

Dam, HULDA.
    Standard.

Sire, Princeps, 536; sire of Trinket, 2:14; Guelph, 2:16½; Greenlander, 2:15¼; Princeton, 2:19¾; Femme Sole, 2:20; Granby, 2:19½; Lucille's Baby, 2:20½; Invincible (4 yrs.), 2:23; and 29 others in 2:30.

2d dam, LADOGA. . . . .
    Sister to Mambrino King, sire of Nightingale, 2:10½; Prince Regent, 2:16½; Mocking Bird, 2:16¾; and 24 others in 2:30.

by MAMBRINO PATCHEN, 58.
    Sire of the dams of Constantine, 2:12½; Ralph Wilkes (2), 2:18; Guy Wilkes, 2:15¼; and 71 others in 2:30.

3d dam, BELLE THORNTON . . .
    Dam of Mambrino King (sire of 27 in the 2:30 list).

by EDWIN FOREST, 49.
    Sire of the dams of So-So, 2:17¼; Mambrino Dudley, 2:19¾; London, 2:20½; and 9 others in 2:30.

4th dam, BROWN KITTY. . . . .
    Dam of Fisk's Mambrino Chief, 2:29½ (sire of Mambrino Sparkle, 2:17; and 4 others in 2:30).

by BIRMINGHAM.
    Thoroughbred son of Stockholder.

5th dam . . . . by BERTRAND.
6th dam . . . . by SUMPTER.
7th dam . . . . by BUZZARD.

Description.—Brown filly, foaled 1892; bred by Graham & Conley, Lexington, Ky. Good size, handsome, and well proportioned, sound, and a very promising way of going.

Arcade Stable

PERFECT VENTILATION,

CLEAN FLOORS,

COMPETENT ATTENDANCE.

Cabs, Carriages, &c.,

AT ALL HOURS.

TELEPHONE No., TREMONT 705.

REAR, 1217 WASHINGTON ST.,

George E. French, Prop.

N. B.   Horses boarded by the day, week, month, or year.

REASONABLE RATES.

No. 6. SIAMESE GIRL.

(Standard.)

Sire,

DON CARLOS, 2097.

Record 2:23.

Sire of Otis Shaw, 2:19¼; Carldon (4), 2:22¼; Alspur, 2:24½; Carlos, 2:27.

Dam, MAY DUDLEY.
Standard.

Sire, Mambrino Dudley, 967; Record, 2:19¾; sire of Crescendo, 2:24; Gretna, 2:22¼; and others in 2:30; and the dams of Alspur, 2:24½; Carlos, 2:27, etc.

2d dam, LADY LAMBERT . . . . by DANIEL LAMBERT, 102.
Dam of Lady Wallace, 2:30¼.

Sire of Comee, 2:19¼; Nancy, 2:23½; Ella Doe, 2:23½; and 33 others in 2:30; and the dams of Pamlico, 2:16¾; Nightingale (p), 2:13½; and 34 others in 2:30.

3d dam . . . . by TI BOY.

Son of Vermont Black Hawk (sire of Ethan Allen, 2:25½; and three others in 2:30).

Description.— Bay filly, foaled 1892; bred by Graham & Conley, Lexington, Ky. Good size, finely made, and good gaited.

23

Park Square Hotel,

(European Plan)

Opposite Providence Depot,   -   -   BOSTON.

Nicely Furnished Rooms by the Day or Week.

G. W. BIXBY, Proprietor.

No. 7.   **PARTHENIA.**

(Standard.)

Sire,

STAMBULA, 11772.

Trial 2:30½; half in 1:12.

Son of Stamboul, 2:07½.

Sire of Murtha, 2:18; Daghestan (2), 2:25½; Redondo (4), 2:23; Sweetwater (2), 2:26; Nadjy, 2:26; Harry Winchester (3), 2:27¼; and 5 others in 2:30.

Dam, WILDBRIAR.
  Four-year record 2:22¾.

Sire, Forrest Glencoe, son of Edwin Forrest; sire of the dams of So-So, 2:17¼; Toney Newell, 2:19¼; Mambrino Dudley, 2:19¾; London, 2:20½; Hermes, 2:27½; and 7 others in 2:30.

2d Dam . . . . by AMERICAN CLAY, 34.
Sire of the dams of David B. (3), 2:19½; Ambassador, 2:21¼; Executor, 2:24¼; Ranchero, 2:24¼; and 24 others in 2:30.

Description.—Bay filly, foaled 1892; bred by Graham & Conley, Lexington, Ky. Fair size, good shape, and promising gaited.

No. 8.   **GENNIE BURKETT.**

(Standard.)

Sire,

DON CARLOS, 2097.

Record 2:23.

Sire of Otis Shaw, 2:19¼; Carldon (4), 2:22¼; Alspur, 2:24½; Carlos, 2:27.

Dam, GENEVE BATES   .   . . .   by GOODWOOD, 2223.
Sire of Greenwood, 2:30; etc.

2d dam, LADY BATES . . . . . .   by YOUNG ETHAN.
Record 2:41.   Son of Ethan Allen, 43; sire of the
dams of 20 in 2:30.

Description.— Bay filly, foaled 1892; bred by Graham & Conley, Lexington, Ky. Extra good size, elegant shape, sound, and well gaited.

No. 9.   INNOCENTIA.

Sire,

IVANEER, 6250.

Son of Electioneer, 125.

Sire of Sunol, 2:08¼ ; Palo Alto, 2:08¾; Arion (3), 2:10½; Truman, 2:12; Norval, 2:14¾; Sweet Rose (1), 2:25¾; Advertiser (3), 2:16; Anteeo, 2:16¼; and 124 others in 2:30.

Dam, KATE TINGLE . . . . by VINDEX.
                                      Sire of the dam of Etta, 2:28½; and son of Blood's Black Hawk; sire of the dam of Almont, Jr.; sire of 23 in 2:30.

2d dam . . . . by DARNABY'S MESSENGER.
                                        Son of Downing's Bay Messenger; sire of Jim Porter, 2:28½ (saddle), etc.

3d dam . . . . by VICTOR.
                                        Son of Downing's Bay Messenger; sire of Jim Porter, 2:28½, etc.

Description.— Chestnut filly, foaled April 20, 1892; bred at Briar Hill Farm, Lexington, Ky. Good size, elegant shape, fine style, and handsome, sound, and a trotting action.

No. 10.   TOREADOR.

(Standard.)

Sire,

IVANEER, 6250.

Son of Electioneer, 125.

Sire of Sunol, 2:08¼; Palo Alto, 2:08¾; Arion (3), 2:10½; Trueman, 2:12; Norval, 2:14¾; Sweet Rose (1), 2:25¾; Advertiser (3), 2:16; Anteeo, 2:16¼; and 124 others in 2:30.

Dam, HURRICANE.
Standard.
                                      Sire, Wedgewood, 692; Record 2:19; sire of Lucille, 2:14½; Favonia, 2:15; Conway (pacer), 2:18¾; Connaught, 2:18¾; Malabar, 2:21¼; Connaught, 2:24; Myrtlewood, 2:25¼; and 10 others in 2:30.

2d dam, DRIVING WIND	by BRIGNOLI, 77.
Trial 2:40 as a four-year-old.	Record 2:29¾. Sire of the dams of King Wilkes, 2:22¼ (sire of Oliver K., 2:16¼); Lady Turpin, 2:23; and 9 others in 2:30.
3d dam, MAY QUEEN	by ETHAN ALLEN, 43.
Dam of May Morning, 2:30 (dam of Revenue, 2:22¼) ; and full sister to Pocahontas, 2:26¾.	Record 2:25½. Sire of Billy Barr, 2:23¾; Hotspur, 2:24; Pocahontas, 2:26¾; and 3 others in 2:30.
4th dam, POCAHONTAS	by CADMUS (Iron's).
Pacing record 2:17½; to wagon in 1855. Dam of Pocahontas, 2:26¾; Tom Rolfe, 2:33½ (sire of Young Rolfe, 2:21¼); May Day (dam of Nancy, 2:23½); May Queen (dam of May Morning, 2:30) ; and Strideaway, 2:31 (sire of Pratt, 2:28).	Sire of Blanco (sire of Smuggler, 2:15¼).
5th dam	by BIG SHAKESPEARE.
6th dam	by BADGER (Probascoe's).

Description.—Black colt foaled 1892, bred by Graham & Conley, Lexington, Ky. Good size, sound, rangy, and good gaited.

No. 11. ALMA WRIGHT.

(Standard.)

Sire,

IVANEER, 6250.

Son of Electioneer, 125.

Sire of Sunol, 2:08¼; Palo Alto, 2:08¾; Arion (3), 2:10½; Truman, 2:12; Norval, 2:14¾; Sweet Rose (1), 2:25¾; Advertiser (3), 2:16; Anteeo, 2:16¼; and 124 others in 2:30.

Dam . . . . by DON WILKES, 2:24¼.
Sire of Capt. John, 2:21¼; Doris, 2:29; and son of Alcyone, sire of Martha Wilkes, 2:08, etc.

2d dam . . . . by WESTWOOD, 2363.
Sire of St. Valentine, 2:16¾; and the dams of Sweetbriar, 2:17½, Blanche Louise (4), 2:15½, etc.

Description.—Bay filly, foaled 1892; bred by Graham & Conley, Lexington, Ky. Fair size, good shape, sound, and good gaited.

No. 12. ALMA TADEMA.

(Standard.)

Out of Katie Jackson, record (4 yrs.) 2:25¾.

Sire,

ALCANTARA, 729.

Record 2:23.

Sire of Chronos, 2:12½; Nightingale, 2:13½; Bayard Wilkes, 2:15; Allen Lowe, 2:16½; Lightning, 2:17; Autograph, 2:17; Miss Alice, 2:17¼; White Locks, 2:20½; and 48 others in 2:30; also the dams of Princess Royal (2), 2:20; Prince Regent, 2:16½; Ægon (3), 2:18½, and others.

Dam, KATIE JACKSON . . . . . . by ALMONT, 33.
Four-year-old record 2:25¾.
Sire of Fanny Witherspoon, 2:16¼; Piedmont, 2:17¼; Westmont (p), 2:13¾; Puritan (p.), 2:16; and 34 others in 2:30; and the dams of Winslow Wilkes, 2:09¾; Alabaster, 2:15; and 58 others in 2:30.

2d dam, FANNY . . . . s. t. b. by IRON'S CADMUS.
Dam of Katie Jackson (4), 2:25¾; Petoskey, sire of Kingtoska (p.), 2:17; Dora Martin (3), 2:19¼; Jewell (4), 2:22½; and 3 others in 2:30.
Sire of Pocahontas (p.), 2:17½; and Blanco (Sire of Smuggler), 2:15¼.

3d dam . . . . s. t. b. by CADMUS.

4th dam . . . . s. t. b. by BROWN'S BELLFOUNDER.

Description.—Alma Tadema is a chestnut filly, foaled 1891; bred at Highlawn Farm, Lee, Mass. Good size, sound, well proportioned, good gaited, and very speedy, and trotted a trial quarter last year, as a yearling, in forty-five seconds.

No. 13. ALICE CLARKE.

Sire,

SENTINEL WILKES, 2499.

Sire of Dashwood, 2:22; Brother G., 2:25¼; Thistle Dew (3), 2:24; Western Wilkes, 2:29¾; and others.

Dam . . . . by MAMBRINO HERO.
Son of Mambrino Patchen, 58. Sire of the dams of Constantine, 2:12½; Crawford (p.), 2:09¾; Riley Medium (p.), 2:10½; Guy Wilkes, 2:15¼; and 80 other standard performers.

2d dam . . . . by HOMER, 1235.
Sire of Lelah H. (4), 2:24½; Vivian, 2:27½; and son of Mambrino Patchen, 58; whose sons have sired the dams of Allerton, 2:09¼; Axtell (3), 2:12; St. Vincent, 2:13½; N. Y. Central, 2:13½, etc.

3d dam . . . . by MARION (THOR).
Son of Lexington, sire of the dam of Ansel, 2:20; and 3 others in 2:30; and g. d. of Jay-Eye-See, 2:06¼, and 2:10; Sunol, 2:08¼, etc.

Description.— Bay filly, foaled 1892, bred by W. H. Crawford, Lexington, Ky. Extra good size, and very handsome shape; smooth and stoutly built, sound, and gaited like a trotter.

No. 14. COLUMBINE.

Sire,

BURLESQUE, 225¼.

Son of Hambrino, 820.

Record 2:21¼.

Sire of Delmarch, 2:11½; Hamdallah, 2:23; Wildbrino, 2:19½; Wilkesbrino, 2:23; and 18 others in 2:30 or better.

Dam, NELL . . . . by DONIPHAN.
2d dam, LUCY . . . . by DARNABY'S TOM.
By Caldwell's Lexington, son of Gist's Black Hawk, by Blood's Black Hawk.

3d dam . . . . by ASHLAND MAMBRINO.
Son of Mambrino Chief.

4th dam . . . . by SCOTT'S HIGHLANDER.
5th dam . . . . by BELT WHIP.

Description.— Bay filly, foaled April 1, 1891; bred by J. J. Coons, Muir, Ky. Good size, handsome and stylish, smoothly put together, sound, a very fast natural pacer, and could show a 40-gait before well broken as a yearling.

PETERS & CALHOUN CO.,

CYNTHIANA HORSE BOOTS,

54 AND 56 SUDBURY ST., BOSTON, MASS.

No. 15.

Sire,

DON CARLOS, 2097.

Record 2:23.

Sire of Otis Shaw, 2:19¼; Carldon (4), 2:22¼; Alspur, 2:24½; Carlos, 2:27, etc.

Dam, GRACE DARLING . . . . . by GOODWOOD, 2223 (trial 2:24½),
Sire of Greenwood, 2:30.

Description.— Chestnut colt, foaled 1892; bred by Graham & Conley, Lexington, Ky. Good size, strong, and stoutly built, smoothly turned, sound, and very good gaited.

No. 16. **HEART'S EASE.**

(Standard.)

Sire,

STAMBULA, 11772.

Trial 2:30½; half in 1:12.

Son of Stamboul, 2:07½.

Sire of Murtha, 2:18; Daghestan (2), 2:25½; Rendodo (4), 2:23; Sweetwater (2), 2:26; Nadjy, 2:26; Harry Winchester (3), 2:27¼; and 5 others in 2:30.

Dam, AGNES WILKES . . . . . . by COMMODORE WILKES, 14197.
Sire of Hardshell (3), 2:28; Coalburg, 2:30, etc., and son of Geo. Wilkes, 519.

2d dam . . . . by TROTTING BOY.
Son of Mambrino Patchen, 58; sire of the dam of Constantine, 2:12½; Ralph Wilkes, 2:13½; Guy Wilkes, 2:15¼; and 80 others in 2:30.

3d dam .   . . . by MAMBRINO PATCHEN, 58.

> The sire of London, 2:20½; and 23 others in 2:30; and the progenitor of 645 trotters with records of 2:30 and better.

4th dam   . . . . . by BENTON'S DIOMED.

5th dam   . . . . . . by GREY EAGLE.

Description.— Brown filly, foaled May 16, 1892; bred at Briar Hill Farm. Good size, fine shape, handsome, and stylish, sound, and very promising.

No. 17. ALLABRIVE.

(Standard.)

Sire,

IVANEER, 6250.

Son of Electioneer, 125.

Sire of Sunol, 2:08¼; Palo Alto, 2:08¾; Arion (3), 2:10½; Truman, 2:12; Norval, 2:14¾; Sweet Rose (1), 2:25¾; Advertiser (3), 2:16; Anteeo, 2:16¼; and 124 others in 2:30.

Dam, LA PERLA . . . . by PILOTEER, 13595.

> Sire of Prize, 2:22¼, and son of Bayard, 53; sire of Kitty Bayard, 2:12¼.

2d dam, KITTY MORRILL . . . . by YOUNG MORRILL, 118.
Out of the g. d. of Faust (3), 2:18¼.

> Sire of Fearnaught, 2:23¼; Mattie Lyle, 2:28, and Draco, 2:28½.

3d dam, LADY KITTREDGE . . . . by C. M. CLAY, Jr., 20.
Dam of Claire, 2:31; dam of Faust (3), 2:18¼.

> Sire of Lady Lockwood, 2:25; Geo. Cooley, 2:27; Lew Sayres, 2:28¾, and Harry Clay, 2:29.

Description.— Bay colt, foaled 1892; bred by Graham & Conley, Lexington, Ky. Good size, strong, and stoutly built, sound, and good gaited.

No. 18. NELL JARLEY.

(Standard.)

Sire,

DON WILKES, 4418.

Record 2:24¾.

Sire of Capt. John, 2:21¼, and Doris, 2:29

Son of Alcyone, 732, sire of Martha Wilkes, 2:08; McKinney, 2:12½; Alcryon, 2:15; Bush, 2:16; Harrietta, 2:18¾; Iona, 2:17½; and 27 others in 2:30.

Dam . . . . by VERMONT WILKES.
      Son of Lyle Wilkes, 4658; sire of
       Wood Wilkes, 2:25; Danville
       Wilkes, 2:27; Konantz, 2:28, etc.

2d dam . . . .
  The g. d. of Wildbriar (4), 2:22¾.

Description.— Black filly, foaled 1892; bred by Graham & Conley, Lexington, Ky. Good size, sound, strong, and compactly built, and good gaited.

2:19¼.   *J. R. SHEDD,*   2:19¼.

The Fastest Son of Red Wilkes in the East.

STANDARD BY BREEDING.   **STANDARD BY PERFORMANCE.**

Sire, Red Wilkes (sire of Prince Wilkes, 2:14¾, Phil Thompson, 2:16¼, and 85 others with records of 2:30 or better).
Dam, Belle Ericsson, by Ericsson (2:30½), son of Mambrino Chief; second dam by Vandal, thoroughbred son of imported Glencoe; third dam by Pilot, Jr.
J. R. SHEDD has a faster trotting record than any other entire son of Red Wilkes, made in a race which he won from Aubine in Buffalo, N. Y., taking the third, fourth, and fifth heats in 2:19½, 2:19¼, 2:20¼.
He has a two-mile four-year-old record of 5:14.
TERMS $100, with the usual return privilege. Send for catalogue and book your mares now.

     Address L. J. STURTEVANT, 15 Union Market, Boston, Mass.
     or R. M. STURTEVANT, Somerville, Mass.

No. 19.   ROSS ALLEN.

Sire,

ALLEN LOWE, 12279.

Record 2:16½.

Son of Alcantara, 729.

Sire of Chronos, 2:12½; Nightingale, 2:13½; Bayard Wilkes; 2:15; Allen Lowe, 2:16½; Lightning, 2:17; Autograph, 2:17; Miss Alice, 2:17¼; White Socks, 2:20½; and 48 others in 2:30.

Dam . . . . by DON CARLOS, 2:23.
      Sire of Otis Shaw, 2:19¼; Carldon,
       2:22¼; Alspur, 2:24½; Carlos,
       2:27.

2d dam . . . . by JUSTIN MORGAN, 2234.
      Sire of Wick, 2:20½; Lady Lowe,
       2:28; and the dam of S and E,
       2:30.

Description.— Bay colt, foaled 1892; bred by Graham & Conley, Lexington, Ky. Good size, sound, well built, and good gaited.

No. 20. **HATTIE PETIT.**

(Standard.)

Sire,

DON CARLOS, 2097.

Record 2:23.

Sire of Otis Shaw, 2:19¼; Carldon (4), 2:22¼; Allspur, 2:24½; Carlos, 2:27.

Dam, TOPSEY
Standard.

Sire, Wedgewood 692; record 2:19; sire of Lucille, 2:14½; Favonia, 2:15; Conway, 2:18¾; Malabar, 2:21¼; Connaught, 2:24; Myrtlewood, 2:25¼; and 10 others in 2:30.

2d dam, TOPSEY . . . . by ETHAN ALLEN, 43.
Sister to Carrie Allen, 2:32.

Record 2:25½. Sire of Billy Barr, 2:23¾; Hotspur, 2:24; Pocahoutas, 2:26¾; and 3 others in 2:30; and the dams of 20 in 2:30.

3d dam, ... by ——
Dam of Carrie Allen, 2:32.

Description.— Bay filly, foaled 1892; bred at Briar Hill Farm, Lexington, Ky. Fair size, sound and shapely, and good gaited.

No. 21. ROSIRA.

(Standard.)

Sire,

IVANEER, 6250.

Son of Electioneer, 125.

Sire of Sunol, 2:08¼; Palo Alto, 2:08¾; Arion (3), 2:10½; Truman, 2:12; Norval, 2:14¾; Sweet Rose (1), 2:25¾; Advertiser (3), 2:16; Anteeo, 2:16¼; and 124 others in 2:30.

Dam, IRIS.
Full sister to Goodwood Jr., record 2:34.

Sire, Goodwood, 2223; trial 2:24; sire of Greenwood, 2:30.

2d Dam, KITTY MORRILL . . . . by YOUNG MORRILL, 118.
Out of the g. d. of Faust (3), 2:18¼.

Sire of Fearnaught, 2:23; Mattie Lyle, 2:28; Draco, 2:28½; and the dams of Matchless, 2:24¾; Volunteer Chief, 2:29½; Nelly, 2:30; and Greenwood, 2:30.

3d dam, LADY KITTRIDGE . . . . s. t. b. by C. M. CLAY, Jr., 20.
The dam of Claire, 2:31, and grandam of Faust, 2:18¼ at three years.

Sire of Lady Lockwood, 2:25; Geo. Cooley, 2:27; Lew Sayres, 2:28¾; and Harry Clay, 2:29.

Description.— Bay colt, foaled 1892; bred by Graham & Conley, Lexington, Ky. Good size, well built, sound, and good gaited.

No. 22. GOLDEN LIGHT.

Sire,

IVANEER, 6250.

Son of Electioneer, 125.

Sire of Sunol, 2:08¼; Palo Alto, 2:08¾; Arion (3), 2:10½; Truman, 2:12; Norval, 2:14¾; Sweet Rose (1), 2:25¾; Advertiser (3), 2:16; Anteeo, 2:16¼; and 124 others in 2:30.

Dam . . . . by HALCORN.

2d dam . . s. t. b. by JOHN DILLARD.
Sire of the dam of Repetition, 2:19¼, and many others.

Description.—Chestnut filly, foaled June 3, 1892; bred at Briar Hill Farm, Lexington, Ky. Extra good size, and nicely shaped filly, strong and stoutly built, sound, and Electioneer gaited.

No. 23.   FRANK STANYAN.

(Standard.)

Sire,

BLACK WILKES, 3541.

Sire of Winslow Wilkes, 2:09¾; Promise, 2:25½; Angelina, 2:29¼.

Dam, BERNICE WILKES	by FAYETTE WILKES, 2036, trial 2:23½. Son of Geo. Wilkes, 519; sire of 79 in 2:30.
2d dam, BERNICE	by HAMBLETONIAN MAMBRINO, 540. Sire of Wild Rake, 2:22¾; Hayden, 2:26½; and 5 others in 2:30.
3d dam, MAGGIE RABBATHEN . .	by MAMBRINO ABDALLAH, 2201. Sire of Mambrino Prince, 2:23¼; Mambrino Bashaw (Sire of Mambrino, 2:27¼); and son of Mambrino Patchen, 58.
4th dam, PATCHEN LASS	by TROTTING BOY. Son of Mambrino Patchen, 58.
5th dam	by MAMBRINO PATCHEN, 58. Sire of the dams of Constantine, 2:12½; Ralph Wilkes (2), 2:18, etc.

Description.—Black colt, foaled 1892; bred by Adams & Vaughan, Lexington, Ky. Good size, sound, good proportion, and good gaited. His breeding is exceptionally high, being a double Wilkes cross on a double Mambrino Patchen.

No. 24.   FRANK PIPER.

Full brother to Precieuse, yearling trial ¼ in thirty-seven seconds.

(Standard.)

Sire,

STAMBULA, 11772.

Trial 2:30½; half in 1:12.

Son of Stamboul, 2:07½.

Sire of Murtha, 2:18; Daghestan (2), 2:25½; Redondo (4), 2:23; Sweetwater (2), 2:26; Nadjy, 2:26; Harry Winchester (3), 2:27¼; and five others in 2:30.

Dam, DEVOTEE.

Standard. Dam of Revolver, trial 2:27; and Precieuse (1), trial ¼ in thirty-seven seconds.	Sire, Pancoast, 1439; record 2:21¾; sire of Ponce de Leon, 2:13; Garnet, 2:13½; Patron, 2:14¼; Prodigal, 2:16; and 12 others in 2:30; and grandsire of Alix, (4) 2:10; Pactolus, 2:12¾, etc.

2d dam, BELLE BOYD . . . . by ABDALLAH, 15.
Record 2:45 as a three-year-old.
Sire of Goldsmith Maid, 2:14; Rosalind, 2:21¾; Thorndale, 2:22¼ (sire of Edwin Thorne, 2:16¼); and 3 others in 2:30; and sire of the dams of 39 in 2:30.

3d dam . . . . by L. I. BLACK HAWK, 24.
Sire of Prince, 2:24½; and Jake Oakley, 2:32½ to wagon in 1856.

Description.— Bay colt, foaled 1892; bred by Graham & Conley, Lexington, Ky. Large size, well made, and very promising. This colt promises as well as his full sister, who is a certain trotter, and went a half last fall as a yearling in 1:19—quarter in 37 seconds—and we expect her to beat 2:30 this year.

No. 25. CHEVALIER BAYARD.

Sire,

IVANEER, 6250.

Son of Electioneer, 125.

Sire of Sunol, 2:08¼; Palo Alto, 2:08¾; Arion (3), 2:10½; Truman, 2:12; Norval, 2:14¾; Sweet Rose (1), 2:25¾; Advertiser (3), 2:16; Anteeo, 2:16¼; and 124 others in 2:30.

Dam, GREY MAC . . . . by BAIR, 1689.
Son of Bayard, 53; Sire of Kitty Bayard, 2:12¼, etc.

2d dam, LADY McBETH. . . . . . by WILKIN'S McBETH.
Son of Mambrino Chief, 11.

Description.— Bay colt, foaled 1892; bred by Graham & Conley, Lexington, Ky. Good size, well put up, sound, and a very promising way of going.

No. 26. COMING SON.

(Standard.)

Sire,

ALLEN LOWE, 12279.

Record 2:16½.

Son of Alcantara, 729.

Record 2:23.

Sire of Chronos, 2:12½; Nightingale, 2:13¼; Bayard Wilkes, 2:15; Allen Lowe, 2:16½; Lightning, 2:17; Autograph, 2:17; Miss Alice, 2:17¼; White Socks, 2:20½; and 48 others in 2:30.

Dam, BELLE ROLFE.
Standard.
Sire, Tom Rolfe, 306; sire of Sleepy Tom (pacer), 2:12¼; Gem (pacer), 2:13¾; Young Rolfe, 2:21¼; sire of Nelson, 2:10; Lady Rolfe, 2:22¼; Tom Rolfe, Jr., 2:22¼; Tom Hendricks, 2:25.

2d dam, WOODSTOCK BELLE .   by WOODSTOCK, 873.
       Sire of Royal John, 2:26¼.

3d dam, LADY DRACO . . . . . .   by BLACK HAWK (Furman's).
   Dam of Draco Prince, 2:24¼.   Son of Vermont Black Hawk (sire
       of Ethan Allen, 2:25½; and 3
       others in 2:30).

Description.— Chestnut colt, foaled 1892; bred by Graham & Conley, Lexington, Ky. Rather small size, nice shape, sound, and compactly built, a natural pacer, with vim and nerve force enough to make a very fast one.

No. 27.   **LADY STANWOOD.**

(Standard.)

Sire,

STAMBULA, 11772.

Son of Stamboul, 2:07½.

Sire of Murtha, 2:18; Daghestan (2), 2:25½; Redondo (4), 2:23; Sweetwater (2), 2:20; Nadjy, 2:26; Harry Winchester (3), 2:27¼; and 5 others in 2:30.

Dam   . . by WEDGEWOOD, 2:19.
       Sire of Lucille, 2:14½; Favonia, 2:15;
       Conway, 2:18¾; Malabar, 2:21¼;
       and 12 others in 2:30.

2d Dam . .   . by ARBITER, 2:22¼
Son of Administrator, 357 ; and the
great Alma Mater, dam of Alcyone,
Alcantara, etc.

Description.— LADY STANWOOD is a brown filly, foaled 1890; bred by
Mr. Winslow, Rockland, Mass., fair size, good proportion, and promising.

No. 28.   HULDA.

(Standard.)

Sire,

PRINCEPS, 536.

Sire of Trinket, 2:14; Greenlander, 2:15¼ ; Guelph, 2:16½ ; Princeton, 2:19¾ ;
Femme Sole, 2:20; Granby, 2:19½ ; Lucille's Baby, 2:20½ ; Invincible (4 yrs.),
2:23; and 29 others in 2:30.

Dam, LADOGA . . . . by MAMBRINO PATCHEN, 58.
Sister to Mambrino King, sire of   Sire of the dams of Ralph Wilkes
Nightingale, 2:10½ ; Prince Re-   (2), 2:18; Tr. 3 yrs., 2:13½ ; Con-
gent, 2:16½ ; Mocking Bird,   stantine, 2:12½ ; Guy Wilkes,
2:10¾ ; and 24 others in 2:30.   2:15¼ ; and 71 others in 2:30.

2d dam, BELLE THORNTON . . . . by EDWIN FORREST, 49.
Dam of Mambrino King (sire of 27   Sire of the dams of So-So, 2:17¼ ;
in the 2:30 list).   Mambrino Dudley, 2:19¾ ; London,
    2:20½ ; and 9 others in 2:30.

3d dam, BROWN KITTY . . . . . by BIRMINGHAM.
Dam of Fisk's Mambrino Chief,   Thoroughbred son of Stockholder.
2:20½ (sire of Mambrino
Sparkle, 2:17 and 4 others in
2:30).

4th dam . . . . by BERTRAND.
5th dam . . . . .   . by SUMPTER.
6th dam . . .   . by BUZZARD.

PRODUCE.

1886—Missed . . . . to DON CARLOS, 2:23.
1887—Missed . . . . to SULTAN, 2:24.
1888—Slipped foal . . . . to DON WILKES, 4418.
1889—Missed . . . . to DON CARLOS, 2097.
1890—Ch. f (died) . . . . by DON CARLOS, 2:23,
1891—Br. f (Viola Harding) sold . . by STAMBULA, 11772.
1892—B. f . . . . by STAMBULA, 11772.
1893—In foal . . . . to CONSTANTINE, 2:12½

Description.—Hulda, foaled 1883, is a bay mare, 16 hands in height; bred
by R. S. Veach, Indian Hill Stock Farm, St. Mathew's, Ky. This is a magnificent
mare individually, large, and justly proportioned, and as she has a rich combination of brood-mare blood, we esteem her very highly.

No. 29.   TOPSEY.

(Standard.)

Sire,

WEDGEWOOD, 692.

Record 2:19.

Sire of Lucille, 2:14½; Favonia, 2:15; Conway, 2:18¾; Malabar, 2:21¼; Connaught, 2:24; Myrtlewood, 2:25¼.

Dam, TOPSEY . . . . by ETHAN ALLEN, 43.
     Sister to Carrie Allen, 2:32.   Record 2:25½; Sire of Billy Barr, 2:23¾; Hotspur, 2:24; Pocahontas, 2:26¾, and three others in 2:30.

2d dam . . . . by ——
     Dam of Carrie Allen, 2:32

PRODUCE.

1889—Blk c . . . . by CHARLEY WILKES, 2:25¼.
1890—Slipped . . .   . . to DON CARLOS, record 2:23.
1891—B. f. (sold)   .   by DON CARLOS, 2:23.
1892—B. f. . . . . by DON CARLOS, 2:23.
1892—Bred . .   . . to DON CARLOS, 2:23.

Description. — Topsey, foaled 1884, is a black mare, bred by Orlando Thompkins, Lexington, Mass. A good-sized, well-formed, and nicely gaited young mare, bred right for either track or breeding purposes. Wedgewood is, without doubt, destined to prove one of the greatest trotting-sires of his generation, and he is just the right kind of a horse to cross with the Ethan Allen family. Bred to Don Carlos, the result ought to be a trotter by right of inheritance at least. Broken to drive.

No. 30. **THORNLEAF.**

(Standard.)

Full sister to Thornburg, 2:21½.

Sire,

JUDGE ADVOCATE, 1263.

Sire of Thornburg, 2:21½; Romulus, 2:24¼; Hortense, 2:26¼.

Son of Messenger Duroc.

Sire of Elaine, 2:20; Prospero, 2:20; Charley Champlin, 2:21¾; Dame Trot, 2:22; John D, 2:23½; Lancelot, 2:23, and 16 others in 2:30.

Dam LADY RENO	by GEN. GRANT.
Dam of Thornburg, 2:21½	Son of Drew Horse (sire of Dirigo, 2:29; Gen. McClellan, 2:29, and Stella, 2:33).
2d dam, FANTINE	by DREW HORSE, 114.
	Sire of the dams of Midnight, 2:18¼; Iron Age, 2:19¼; Volunteer Maid, 2:27; Minnie Moulton, 2:27¼, and Iolanthe, 2:30.

PRODUCE.

1888—Missed	to BERMUDA, 2:20½.
1891—B. F. ROSELEAF	by MYRTLEWOOD, 2:25¼.
1892—Ch. c.	by DON CARLOS, 2:23.
1892—Bred	to DON CARLOS, 2:23.

Description.—THORNLEAF, foaled 1885, is a bay mare; bred by J. M. Littlefield, Foxcroft, Me. This is a full sister to the fast gelding, Thornburg, 2:21½, and should prove valuable as a brood-mare, as producing blood is so much in demand.

No. 31. **MISS WILLIAMS.**

Sire,

BRYANT W.

Full brother to Molly McCarthy, the great race mare.

Dam	by NUTWOOD, 2:18¼, 600.
	Sire of Manager (4), 2:09¾; Lockheart, 2:13; Nuthurst, 2:14¾; Nutpine, 2:15½; and 97 others in 2:30; and the dams of Arion (3), 2:10½; Sabledale (2), 2:18½; and 30 others in 2:30.
2d dam	by WILLIAMSON'S BELMONT.
A great road mare that trialed in 2:31.	Sire of Venture, 2:27¼; and the dams of Nimrod, 2:19¾; Belle Echo, 2:20; Prince, 2:23¾; Bob Mason, 2:27¼; and 4 others in 2:30.

Description.— Miss Williams is bay mare, with star and snip, foaled 1885; bred by Mr. Thomas Williams, San Francisco, Cal. Fine size, very elegant conformation, smooth, sound, and good gaited. Broken double.

She has two colts now in the hands of Mr. John Goldsmith, one by Guy Wilkes, 2:15½, and the other by Sidney, 2:19¾; and Mr. Goldsmith writes us that he is just breaking the latter and expects that she will make a trotter from the way she promises now. Miss Williams also has a yearling filly by Constantine, 2:12½, that is an elegant individual and *very* good gaited and promising. There is little doubt but what this mare will be a producing dam very soon. She is in foal to Empire Wilkes, 2:30, which cross should prove a very happy one.

Consignment of Wm. Kelley, South Boston, Mass.

No. 32. MOLLY K.

(Standard.)

Sire,

IVANEER, 6250.

Son of Electioneer, 125.

Sire of Sunol, 2:08¼; Palo Alto, 2:08¾; Arion (3), 2:10½; Truman, 2:12; Norval, 2:14¾; Sweet Rose (1), 2:25¾; Advertiser (3), 2:16; Anteeo, 2:16¼; and 124 others in 2:30.

Dam, ROSADONNA . . . . . . by DON WILKES, 4418; record 2:24¾.
Sire of Capt. John, 2:21½; and Doris, 2:20; and son of Alcyone; sire of Martha Wilkes, 2:08.

2d dam, BRIAR ROSE.
Standard.
Sire Joe Downing, 710; sire of dam of Lorene, 2:15¼; Abe Downing, 2:20¾; dam of Rarely, 2:24½; dam of Jewess, 2:26; Dick Jamison, 2:26; dam of Ky. Hambletonian, 2:27.

3d dam, GOODMAN MARE . . . . by ERICSSON, 130.
Sire of Rarely, 2:24½; Doble, 2:28; Eric, 2:28¼; as a four-year-old, and three others in 2:30.

4th dam . . . . by BERTRAND.

Description.—Molly K. is a black filly, foaled April 6, 1891; bred by Wm. Kelly, South Boston, Mass. Fair size, nicely shaped, and a *sure* trotter if there ever was one; was broken as a yearling, and showed as much speed as any yearling ever on Briar Hill Farm. When barely broken showed quarter in forty-five seconds, but went wrong soon after and was obliged to be turned out; with proper handling she is sure to develop into a very fast mare.

No. 33.   ARENA.

(Standard.)

Sire,

STAMBULA, 11772.

Trial, 2:30½; half in 1:12.

Son of Stamboul, 2:07½.

Sire of Martha, 2:18; Daghestan (2), 2:25½; Redonda (4), 2:23; Sweetwater (2), 2:26; Nadjy, 2:26; Harry Winchester (3), 2:27¼; and 5 others in 2:30.

Dam, ROSADONNA . . . . . . by DON WILKES, 4418; record 2:24¾.
Sire of Capt. John, 2:21½; and Doris, 2:29; and son of Alcyone, sire of Martha Wilkes, 2:08.

Description.— Bay colt, foaled March 12, 1892; bred by Wm. Kelly, South Boston, Mass. Extra good size, strong, and stoutly built, sound, and very promising gaited.

Consignment of J. J. Coons, Muir, Ky.

No. 34.   KENELM.

Sire,

IVANEER, 6250.

Son of Electioneer, 125.

Sire of Sunol, 2:08¼; Palo Alto, 2:08¾; Arion (3), 2:10½; Truman, 2:12; Norval, 2:14¾; Sweet Rose (1), 2:25¾; Advertiser (3), 2:16; Anteeo, 2:16¼; and 124 others in 2:30.

Dam, NEB   . . . by FAYETTE CHIEF, 8894.
Sire of King Herod, 2:16½; and son of Mambrino King, 1279.

2d dam   . . by SIR WESTLY, son of Washington Denmark.

3d dam .   by DONIPHAN.

Description.— Bay colt, foaled May 8, 1892; bred at Briar Hill Farm, Lexington, Ky., good size, well put up, rangy, and bloodlike, sound and *very* good gaited, and promising.

No. 35.

DR. SIMMONS.

Sire,

BLACK CHIEF.

Son of Mambrino Chief, 11.

Sire of Lady Thorn, 2:18¼; Woodford Mambrino, 2:21½; dam of Director, 2:17 (sire of 18 in 2:30); dam of Onward, 2:25¼; sire of 65 in 2:30; Mambrino Patchen, 58; sire of 24 in 2:30; and the dams of 83 in 2:30.

Dam, BEAUTY . . . . by REVEILLE, 1472.
Record 2:21¼. Sire of Rinaldo, 2:27; Revolt (3), 2:22¾; Harry Baldwin, 2:24½; Linnette, 2:28¼; etc.

2d dam . . . . by BLACK SNAKE.

Description.— Dr. Simmons is a black gelding, foaled 1889, bred by Dr. Simmons, Lexington, Ky., good size, good shape, sound and kind. Well broken to ride and drive, afraid of nothing and can show considerable speed, and will make a great road or general purpose horse.

Consignment of Estate of John B. Clarke.

No. 36.

ELECTIONHER.

Brown filly, foaled June 8, 1892.

(Standard and registered, A. T. R.)

BY

FALLIS, 2:23.

(Sire of Fal Rose and 3 others in 2:30) by Electioneer (sire of 132 from 2:08¼; 31 from 2:08¼ to 2:20; 28 speed-getting sons and 24 dams of speed); dam Felicia, by Messenger Duroc.

Dam, STARLETTE . . . . by STEELE, 1556.
Steel gray mare, foaled 1888.
Sire of Arago, Puritan, etc., by Startle; dam Hebe by the great Belmont.

2d dam, NELLIE WILKES . . . . by MAMBRINO WILKES, 2:28¾.
Sire of Arthur Wilkes, 2:19; Mischief, 2:24¾; R. M. Wilkes, 2:25¼, etc., by George Wilkes, 5:19, 2:22; dam by Williams' Mambrino.

3d dam, FANNY LYON . . . . . by GENERAL LYON, 493.
Sire of Richmond, 2:26, etc. Sire of
the dams of 3, by Morrill, 850.

4th dam, SHERMAN MORGAN MARE

Description. — Electionher is one of the best bred fillies in New England, and, individually, is as good as her breeding. Fallis is conceded to be one of the very best sons of the great Electioneer, from whatever standpoint considered, and Electionher is a credit to her sire. She has good color, splendid size, and a trotting gait that will land her ahead of the money. She will grow to be a grand brood-mare. No better blood lines can be asked than those contained in this filly ? The blood of Electioneer, George Wilkes, Belmont, and American Star are all there, with other rich strains, in hot quantities, and, with an individual built right to propel them, there can be but one result,— a trotter and a race horse.

No. 37.   STARLETTE.

Steel-gray mare, foaled 1888; standard and registered, A. T. R.

BY

STEELE, 1556.

Sire of Arago, 2:22½; Puritan, 2:25, etc.; by Startle, 200; sire of Instant, 2:14½; Majolica, 2:15, etc.; sire of Mambrino Startle, sire of Mambrino Maid, 2:15¼; and grandsire of the world's champion five-year-old race trotter, Belle Vard, 2:08¾.

Dam, NELLIE WILKES . . . . . by MAMBRINO WILKES, 2:28¾.
Sire of Arthur Wilkes, 2:19 (the
fastest New Hampshire bred trotter); Mischief, 2:24¾; R. M. Wilkes,
2:25¼, etc.; son of George Wilkes,
519, 2:22; dam by Williams' Mambrino.

2d dam, FANNY LYON . . . . . by GENERAL LYON, 493.
Sire of Richmond, 2:26, etc.; sire of
dams of 3; by Morrill, 850.

3d dam, SHERMAN MORGAN MARE.

Description.— Here is a right good young mare, and a sure enough trotter if she gets the chance. The Wilkes-Belmont cross has rarely failed to produce trotters, and this particular nick has been very successful. The New Hampshire bred four-year-old, Bonner Steele, is bred just like Starlette. This colt could trot in 2:30 last fall, and was the winner last winter of a hotly contested seven heat race over the ice at Concord, N. H., against a field of aged horses. He is one of the best gaited and gamest colts ever raised in New England, and Starlette possesses all of his nerve and vim, and, I think, will go as fast. She has never been trained, having produced a foal last year (next number in the Catalogue) and is due to foal this summer to the grand young stallion, Fire King, 17638, a fashionably bred grandson of Lord Russell, brother to Maud S., 2:08¾, and sire of the world's champion race stallion, Kremlin, 2:07¾. Starlette should beat 2:30 the first season she is trained.

No. 38.　　　　　JOLLY JINGLES.

Bay colt, foaled May 25, 1892.

Bred by W. H. Jones, Garfield, Vt.

BY

JINGLES, 14872, 2:28¾.

(Son of Baron Wilkes, 2:18; sire of Brava, 2:14½; Margrave (2), 2:19¼, and 16 others; the champion sire of his age; dam Lamberta (a producer) by Daniel Lambert.

Dam . . . . by PLOW BOY.
　　　　　　　　　　　　　Grandson of Morrill, 850.
　　　　　　　　　　　　　Sire of 8 speed getters.

2d dam . . . . s. t. b. by WOODBURY MORGAN.
　　　　　　　　　　　　　Son of Justin Morgan, founder of the Morgan family.

Description. — Here is a colt that all lovers of Morgan horses will want to take a good look at. The Morgan nerve and style is all here in an individual that will make his mark on the track and road. His dam is a direct descendant of the founder of the great Morgan family, through Old Morrill, grandson of Young Bulrush Morgan, on one side, and Woodbury Morgan, son of Justin Morgan, on the other. She has been one of the toughest and speediest road-mares ever raised in Vermont, and her imprint has been indelibly placed upon this colt. Jingles, the sire of Jolly Jingles (that, by the way, is the oldest of his get) is a son of Baron Wilkes, 2:18, one of the stoutest bred and gamest race horses in the whole Wilkes family. At the age of ten years he is the sire of eighteen standard performers, including the great stake-winning two-year-old Margrave, 2:19¼, and takes rank as the champion ten-year-old sire. The dam of Baron Wilkes was Belle Patchen, 2:30¾, by Mambrino Patchen, and his grandam was Sally Chorister (dam of Proteine, 2:18, Belle Brasfield, 2:20, etc.), by Mambrino Chorister, son of Mambrino Chief. This is hot stuff, and is the kind of blood the market is paying for.

Consignment of J. W. Ellsworth.

No. 39.　　　　　DOCTOR.

Black gelding, foaled July 31, 1889.

Bred by Walter Flagg, Worcester, Mass; owned by J. W. Ellsworth.

BY

CROMWELL PRINCE.

By Cromwell, 9979, 2:36½, the sire of Baby S, 2:24½; Cromwell, Jr., 2:27½; Bright-wood, 2:29½, and many others with records, 2:30.

Dam, MORGAN MARE . . . . . . Pedigree not traced.
　　Was a good, sound mare and could go in 2:50.

Description. — This is a handsome black colt with long tail; stands close to 15½ hands high, weighs about 950, good styled, speedy formed colt with best of action and lots of speed, and with a little handling will go fast; is sound and kind; broke to both single and double harness, and is worthy the attention of good horsemen.

No. 40.   GLENBELLE.

(Standard).

Gray roan filly, foaled April 5, 1890.

Bred and owned by J. W. Ellsworth.

BY

GLENWOOD, 12403.

Son of Nutwood, 600, dam, Tipsey, by Alcalde, 103.

Dam, KAZETA	by CASSIUS M. CLAY, JR., 22.
Dam of Silver King, 2:38½.	Sire of 4; 10 sons with 31; 26 dams of 32.
2d dam, KATE THOMPSON	by ERICSSON, 130.
Dam of Rampart, 2:36.	Sire of 6; 3 speed-getting sons; 12 dams of 13.
3d dam, LADY GOODWIN	by BURR'S COLUMBUS.
4th dam	by ABDALLAH I.

Description.—Roan filly; star and feather; 15¼ hands high; weight, 900 pounds. Glenbelle is a superb filly individually as well as by breeding; she was broken in her yearling form and showed quarters in 46 seconds; last year she was not used. This winter, however, she has been used to sleigh some, and shows speed enough to warrant the prediction that she will trot in 2:30 this year. She is beautifully gaited and an extra good road mare. Her first and second dams produced Silver King, 2:38½, and Rampart, 2:36, respectively. She is very highly finished, stylish, and handsome, and will show for herself on day of sale.

No. 41.   ALCAZETA.

(Standard.)

Bay filly, foaled March 15, 1891.

Bred and owned by J. W. Ellsworth.

BY

ALCANTARA (4), 723, 2:23.

Sire of 51 from 2:12½; 12 speed getters; 5 dams of 7.

Dam, KAZETA	by CASSIUS M. CLAY, JR., 22.
Dam of Silver King, 2:38½.	Sire of 4; 10 sons with 31; 26 dams of 32.
2d dam, KATE THOMPSON	by ERICSSON, 130.
Dam of Rampart, 2:36.	Sire of 6; 3 speed-getting sons; 12 dams of 13.
3d dam, LADY GOODWIN	by BURR'S COLUMBUS.
4th dam	by ABDALLAH I.

Description.—Small star; left hind pastern white; 15 hands high; weighs about 900 pounds; broken the past winter. She is a typical Alcantara in every respect; very speedy and with handling will learn to go fast. She won the first premium last year at the N. E. Fair over 23 competitors. It is needless to eulogize on the merits of her size. Her dam, Kazeta, has produced Silver King, four-year-old race record 2:38½; and her second dam produced Rampart, 2:36. Alcantara fillies are seldom on the market at any price, and this is a rare chance to secure a first-class one; she is large and handsome, with the best of feet and legs, and is warranted sound.

No. 42.   PURE WILKES FILLY.

(Standard.)

Brown filly, foaled April 17, 1892.

Bred and owned by J. W. Ellsworth.

BY

PURE WILKES, 18897, 2:29.

Son of Red Wilkes, the greatest son of George Wilkes; dam Purity, a great producing mare by Brignoli.

Dam, KAZETA . . . . by CASSIUS M. CLAY, JR., 22.
    Dam of Silver King, 2:38½.   Sire of 4; 10 sons with 31; 26 dams of 32.

2d dam, KATE THOMPSON . . . by ERICCSON, 130.
    Dam of Rampart, 2:36.   Sire of 6; 3 speed getters; 12 dams of trotters.

3d dam, LADY GOODWIN . . by BURR'S COLUMBUS.

4th dam . . . . by ABDALLAH I.

Description.—Dark brown, black points; this filly is a grand individual and a well-bred one. She is finely gaited, broken to halter, and leads very fast; her sire is acknowledged one of the best sires of early speed in New England; and her first and second dams have produced race horses; she has good size, the best of feet and legs, and if trained will make a sure yearling stake winner next fall; perfectly straight and sound in every way.

No. 43.   WHIPPLE.

Bay gelding, foaled May 7, 1890; bred and owned by J. W. Ellsworth.

BY

WHIPSTER, 13478.

Son of Whips, 13407, by Electioneer; dam, Maybird, by St. Clair, 656.

Dam, FLY . . . . by RICHWOOD, 5323.
    Has shown a mile in 2:34.   Sire of Jennie, 2:21¾; and 7 others in the list.

2d dam, VELOCIPEDE . . . by NED SARGENT.
    A fast road mare.   Son of Nonpareil.

3d dam . . . .
    Thoroughbred.

Description.—Solid cherry bay; 15½ hands high; weight, about 1,000 pounds. This is one of the finest young geldings that can be found. His size, gait, and conformation are all that can be desired in a gentleman's driving horse. He was broken as a yearling, and showed quarters under 50 seconds. As a two-year-old he was castrated and was not used. He has been driven the past winter to sleigh, and can now speed a 30 gait, and will trot fast this year if handled. Absolutely sound and kind in every respect.

No. 44.   KNEELAND.

(Standard.)

Bay colt, foaled May 1, 1892; bred by Chas. Backman, Esq.; owned by J. W. Ellsworth.

BY

LELAND, 1300.

Sire of Geneva, 2:14, and 6 other race horses; by Hambletonian, 10; dam, Imogene, the dam of Arthurton.

Dam, MINETTO . . . . by KENTUCKY PRINCE, 2470.
  Dam of Blondette, two-year-old   Sire of 26 from 2:10¼; 10 sons with
  record, 2:36¼.   44; 8 dams of 10.

2d dam, MINEOLA . . . . by HAMBLETONIAN, 10.
  Sister to Banker (sire of Bermuda,   Sire of 40; 138 sons with 1182; 69
  2:20.)   dams of 91.

3d dam, LADY BANKER . . . . . by ROE'S ABDALLAH CHIEF.
  Dam of Banker (sire of Bermuda,
  2:20).

4th dam . . . . by SALTRAN.

5th dam . . . .
  Thoroughbred.

Description.— Light bay; star and white hind ankles. This is a finely bred colt with rich speed inheritance, fine appearing, and good gaited; broken to halter and leads fast. His full sister, Blondette, has a two-year-old race record of 2:36¼, and last year, as a three-year-old, she showed a mile in 2:25, with repeat in 2:24¼, and this colt will be equally as fast at the same age.

Consignment of John E. Thayer.

No. 45.   SISTER B.

(Full sister to Tiny B. (3), 2:34¼; race record, 2:26¼.)

Bay mare; foaled 1890.

Bred by Burlen & Finn, Union Springs, N. Y.

BY

CHARLEY B., 2:25.

(Sire of 16 square-gaited trotters in the list) by Champion, 807; dam by Magnum Bonum.

Dam, PAULINE . . . . by PRINCE IMPERIAL.
  Dam of Tiny B., 2:26½; Douglas   Son of Flora Temple, 2:19¾.
  (3), 2:41½.

2d dam, BECKY SHARP . . . . . by BILLY DENTON, 65.
Son of Hambletonian, 10; dam by
Exton Eclipse. He sired John
Love, 2:28½, and Captain, 2:28;
two of his sons sired trotters, and
his daughter produced Nino, 2:30.

3d dam, KENT MARE . . . . . . by LONG ISLAND BLACK HAWK, 24.
Son of Andrew Jackson, 4; dam
Sally Miller, 2:27, by Tippoo Saib.
He sired Prince, 2:24½; Jake
Oakley (wagon), 2:32½. Seven
sons sired 15, and his daughters
produced Lady Mack, 2:25¼, and
three others.

4th dam . . . . by ABDALLAH I.
Son of Mambrino; dam Amazonia.
He sired Sir Walter, 2:27, and
three others; his daughters produced Goldsmith Maid, 2:14, and
6 others, and his son, Hambletonian 10, needs no introduction.

Description. — This is a sweetly gaited filly, stands 15 hands; sound and
broken to single and double harness. She ought to be a trotter, and as fast as
her sister which is to be campaigned this year and should lower her present
record. Here is a bargain for some one that can buy a mate to her. It will take
a good team to beat such a pair on track or road.

Consignment of A. B. Forbes.

No. 46. CALLISTE.

Chestnut filly, foaled March 27, 1891.

Bred by A. B. Forbes.

BY

CALLISTO, 10748, 2:35.

(Son of Alcantara; dam, Annie Page, by Daniel Lambert, 102.)

Dam, LA TOSCA . . . . by WILLIAM TELL, 1692.
Son of Knickerbocker, 200; dam
Gossip, by Mambrino Patchen, 58.

2d dam, LADY HOE . . . . . . by ROBERT BONNER, 270, 2:33.
Sire of 2; 6 sons with 11; and the
dams of 4.

3d dam, HOE MARE. . . . . . . by WILSON'S SIR HENRY.
4th dam . . . . by CROCKER'S ECLIPSE.
5th dam . . . . by RED BIRD.

Description. — Calliste is a chestnut filly, no white. She is perfectly sound.
She has been driven double and shows better than a three-minute clip. She has
been driven single a few times and is a grand roadster.

No. 47. **VELOS.**

Bay gelding, foaled March 8, 1891; bred by A. B. Forbes.

BY

LOMBARDY, 4901.

Son of Clairmont, 2420; dam Ballot, by Electioneer.

Dam, VARA . . . . by LARKIN, 3070.
Son of Sir Walkill; sire of 7; dam, Anna, by Victor, 937.

2d dam, ANN AUGUSTA . . . . . . by UNCAS CHIEF.
Son of Hambletonian, 10.

3d dam, ANNA . . . . by VICTOR.
Son of Cassius M. Clay.

4th dam, LADY LARKIN . . . . . by LITTLE JACK.
Son of L. I. Black Hawk.

5th dam . . . . by LONG ISLAND BLACK HAWK.

Description.— This is a dark bay, no white, of good size and perfectly sound. He has been driven double with Vardy (see next entry). Has never been handled for speed, but shows a good gait.

No. 48. **VARDY.**

Bay gelding, foaled Feb. 28, 1890; bred by A. B. Forbes.

BY

LOMBARDY, 4901.

Son of Clairmont, 2420; dam, Ballot, by Electioneer.

Dam, VARA . . . . by LARKIN, 3070.
Son of Sir Walkill; sire of 7; dam, Anna, by Victor, 937.

Description.— Mate to full brother, preceding entry. Dark bay gelding with black points; no white. Good size and perfectly sound. He has not been handled for speed.

No. 49.   HIGHLARK.

Chestnut colt, foaled May 22, 1892.

Bred by A. B. Forbes.

BY

LARKIN, 3070.

(Son of Sir Walkill, sire of 7; dam, Anna, by Victor, 937.)

Dam. HIATOGA BELLE	by BILLY GREEN.
Trial, 2:24½.	Son of Scott's Hiatoga; sire of 9; 4 sons that have sired speed; 11 dams of 13.
2d dam	by HAUDLEY'S HIATOGA.
3d dam	by QUINN'S TUCKAHOE.
4th dam	by INBRED CONSUL.

Description.— This is a chestnut with two white hind pasterns and small strip in face. He is a natural pacer in the lot but has not been broken.

No. 49 A.   SYPHAX.

Bay colt, foaled 1889; bred by A. B. Forbes.

BY

NOMINEE, 4150, 2:21¼.

Combination of the blood lines of Goldsmith Maid, Lucy, Jay Gould, Lady Thorn, George M. Patchen, and General Knox.

Dam, FAWN	by ABRAHAM, 353.
Three fourths sister to Ella Doe, 2:23¼.	2 in 2:20; 7 in 2:30; dams of Hustler, 2:20½; Ketch, 2:18¾.
2d dam, STICKNOSE	by COLUMBUS, 1703.
Dam of Ella Doe, 2:23¼.	Son of Young Columbus, 95.
3d dam, GRANDAM OF ELLA DOE .	by COLUMBUS, 95.
	Sire of 11; 6 sires of 19; 8 dams of 9.
4th dam, FANNY COOK	by ABDALLAH I.
Dam of Daniel Lambert and Ethan Allen.	Sire of 3; 1 with 40; 7 dams of trotters.
5th dam	by AMERICAN STAR.
6th dam	by RED BIRD.
	Son of Bishop's Hambletonian.

Description.— This fellow is certainly entitled to show speed if there is any virtue in the law of heredity. A notable peculiarity in the breeding of his sire is that in four generations of his tabulated pedigree not one non-standard animal is found, thus making him nearly a thoroughbred trotter. There are very few indeed in the whole country of horses so purely bred in standard lines as is Nominee. Syphax's dam, Fawn, is three fourths sister to Ella Doe, 2:23¼, and is equally speedy, but being less controllable has never taken a record. His second dam, Sticknose, is a producing mare. His fourth dam, Fanny Cook, is the dam of two producing sons. He could show one fourth in forty-five seconds as a three-year-old. He is 15½ hands high, and sound. Here is a bargain. He is of good size, and a grand individual.

Consignment of E. C. Graves.

No. 50.   SEA BREEZE.

(Standard.)

Black filly, foaled 1888.

Owned and bred by Edward C. Graves, 35 Hawkins Street, Boston, Mass.

Standard bred.

BY

BLACKWOOD (3), 74, 2:31.

(Sire of Proteine, 2:18; and 6 others in the list; 8 speed getters and 14 dams
of 19), by Norman, 25; dam by Mambrino Chief, 11.

Dam, ROSA, 2d . . . . by ARISTOS, 771; 2:27¾.
                                   Sire of 14 in the list; 5 speed getters;
                                   dams of 3.

2d dam ROSA . . . . by BROWN HARRY, 799.
                                   Sire of Cora F., Jennie W., and St.
                                   Elmo. Dams of Emma B. and
                                   Pearl.

Description.— Black mare, with small white star, about 15¼ hands, foaled
April 28, 1888; partially broken single; proved kind and good gaited. She was bred
as a three-year-old to Eldorado 10700 by Guy Wilkes. She foaled a fine colt last
summer and was ordered bred back to the same horse, but through a misunder-
standing the instructions were not carried out. Daughters of Blackwood have
produced eighteen trotters in the 2:30 list and his blood is highly prized on the
best stock farms in the country. In Sea Breeze this favorite brood-mare cross
is backed up by Morgan blood through two of the best families of that strain,
and she will prove a valuable addition to the harem of any breeder.

Consignment of J. W. Brodbine.

No. 51.   BILLY BIRD, 10149, 2:26¼.

Roan horse, foaled 1886.

Property of J. W. Brodbine, Boston.

BY

JAY BIRD, 5060.

Sire of 5060; sire of 25 trotters from 2:09¼; 2 sons that have sired speed from
a three-year-old in 2:11¼; and the dam of Courrier, 2:30.

Dam, EMMA G. . . . . by ALMONT, 33, 2:39¼.
   Dam of Billy Bird, 2:26¼; Molly   Sire of 37, from 2:13¼: 75 sons with
   Bird, 2:25.   269; 49 daughters with 67 from
                                         2:09¾.

2d dam, MADAM FINCH . . . . . by MAWPIN'S DRENNON.
    Dam of Jim Finch, 2:25; and a   Sire of the dam of Jim Finch and a
    great brood-mare.   producer of 2 in the list.

3d dam, MADAM FINCH'S DAM . . by GENERAL TAYLOR.
        Sire of General Taylor, 2d; sire of
        dams of 2 in the list.

Description.—This grand race horse requires no commendation in New England. He has been owned, trained, and driven by an amateur who weighs two hundred pounds, and who does not claim to be expert. He started this horse eight time and won four first moneys. He never won a heat that he did not win the race, and he forced Huldy B. to her mark of 2:21¾. Look up the Year Book on this fellow and take into consideration his chances, and you will make up your mind he is a cheap horse at any price. We sold great horses last year but here is the best race horse of the lot.

Consignment of D. W. Blanchard.

No. 52.   HOMERE.

Chestnut horse, foaled 1885.

Bred by the French Government.

Description.— This imported French roadster stallion is of a bright chestnut color, stands 16 hands, and weighs 1250 pounds. Was bred by the French Government at Robour's Department of L'Orne, France, May 20, 1885. He is the finest type of the high-bred horse, being trappy-gaited as a pony, with a vigorous constitution, strong nerve, and extreme stylish action; is a perfect type of the well-known Morgan breed of horses. He not only possesses speed, courage, and endurance, and a perfect disposition, but is capable of roading twelve to fifteen miles an hour, and can trot a mile better than three minutes. He was imported for stud service only; is a sure foal getter. His colts are extra fine, and worthy of attention, a few of which are owned by Col. John E. Thayer, who can be referred to. Homere was awarded first premium at the Bay State Fair, 1889.

No. 53.   REFUND.

Refund, the racing thoroughbred stallion, was foaled 1885; color, chestnut; stands 16 hands. Bred by R. W. Walden, Bowling Brook Stud, Maryland. By "Sensation," he by "*Imp. Leamington*," and 1st dam, "Susie Beane," by "*Lexington*"; 2d, Sally Lewis," by "*Imp. Glencoe*"; and 3d, "Motto," by "Imp. Barefoot." *Refund's dam was "Letty" by "Imp. Australian"*; 2d, "Little Miss," by "Imp. Sovereign"; 3d, "Little Mistress," by "Imp. Shamrock"; 4th, "Glance," by "Wild Bill"; 5th, "Grey Goose," by "Pacolet"; 6th, "Sally Sneed," by "Imp. Buzzard"; 7th, "Jane Hunt," by "Wade Hampton Paragon"; 8th, mare by "Imp. Figure"; 9th, "Miss Slamerkin," by "Imp. Wildare"; 10th, "Imp. Cub Mare," by "Cub"; 11th, "Amaranthus," dam by "Second."

Description.— Refund is royally bred, good disposition, has the size and substance to make a grand stallion for stock purposes; he can carry any weight and has won races in the fastest company from 5-8 mile to 1 1-2 miles. Can be fitted to race at short notice. Refund met with an accident when a two-year-old, causing bunch on ankle, which never interfered with his racing. Would make a great stock horse to cross with trotting-mares. The story that has been told by the infusion of these bloodlines is told in the production of Maud S., Jay-Eye-See, Martha Wilkes, Kremlin, Moquette, Greenleaf, and most of the champion harness horses.

No. 54.   MAGOG PRINCE, 20822.

Bay colt, foaled July 15, 1890.

Property of D. W. Blanchard.

BY

ABDALLAH WILKES, 7562,

Sire of Saxon, 2:22½, and Voleta, 2:26¾.

Dam, BLACK PRINCESS . . . . . by MAMBRINO PATCHEN, 58.
   Dam of Fred Wilkes, 2:26¼.   Sire of 22; 39 sons with 100; 65 dams of 82.

2d dam, LADY BUGG . . . . . . by STAR DAVIS.

3d dam, LIZZIE BUGG . . . . . . by EPSILON.

4th dam, COTTAGE GIRL. . . . . Strictly thoroughbred.

Description. — This is a solid colored bay of good size. Though a late foal he is of good size and shows natural ability at the trot. He will show for himself. He is bred exactly like Ralph Wilkes, being by a son of George Wilkes, out of a Mambrino Patchen mare; second dam, thoroughbred.

No. 55.   ISONOMY.

Cherry bay gelding, foaled April 9, 1889.

Bred by Graham and Conley.

BY

IVANEER, 6250.

(For full description see front of catalogue in Graham & Conley's consignment.)

Dam, GOLDEN SLIPPER . . . , . by IMP. GLENELG.

2d dam, LITTLE KIT . . . . . . by STAR DAVIS, JR.

3d dam, OLD KIT . . . . by BOSTON.

Description. — This is a stylish, handsome, well-shaped colt, bred in Palo Alto style. He is a sure trotter. Hiram Woodruff drove him last fall in 2:42, last half in 1:19, with only a few weeks' handling. He is clever and safe for anyone to drive. This is a good one and a trotter.

Consignment of Payne Stock Farm, Hinsdale, Mass.

For reference only.

WILLIAM TELL, 1692.

Brother in blood to Tribune, 2:25¼.

Bay horse, foaled May 11, 1880.

Owned by L. M. Payne, Hinsdale, Mass.

BY

KNICKERBOCKER, 200.

(By Hambletonian, 10; dam, Lady Patchen, by Geo. M. Patchen.)

Sire of 10 trotters; 6 speed getters; dams of Chronos, 2:12½, and 6 others.

Dam, GOSSIP . . . . by MAMBRINO PATCHEN, 58.
    Dam of Altus, 2:30.   Full brother to Lady Thorne, 2:18¼.
                                 Sire of 22 trotters; 30 sires of 100;
                                 65 dams of 82 in list.

2d dam, PRECEPTRESS . . . . . by CASSIUS M. CLAY, JR., 22, 2:35¼.
                                 Sire of 4; 10 sons with 31; 26 dams
                                 of 34 from 2:18¼.

3d dam, thoroughbred . . . . . . by BERTRAND.
                                 Son of Sir Archy, by Imp. Diomed.

Description. — This brother in blood to Tribune, five-year-old record 2:25¼, is a dark mahogany bay, star, off hind foot white. Foaled May 11, 1880; stands 16¼ hands high, weight in stud condition, 1300 lbs. William Tell was winner of the first prize at New England Fair, Worcester, Mass., Sept. 5, 1882; Pittsfield and Adams fairs, 1882; Pittsfield fair, 1883; and winners of first prize at the National Horse Show, New York, Oct. 22, 1883, and awarded first prize at Bay State Fair, Springfield, Mass., Oct., 1888, always getting first prize wherever shown. William Tell is all that could be expected from such magnificent race-horse breeding. He is as fine a looking stallion as can be found, is a natural trotter, starts off on a trot, does not hitch or hobble, does not require boots or weights, is a fast walker, and a great road horse. He will not only sire speed, but size, and looks as well. He has never been a season out of the stud, was handled a very little one fall, and trotted over a half mile track in 2:31¼. Only two of his colts foaled at the Payne Stock Farm have been handled and but little; they trotted on a half-mile track as two-year-olds in 2:50, one of them winning a race and taking a record in 3:08¼. She was then put to breeding; the other, a stallion, has been in the stud ever since, and trotted last year a half mile in 1:10 as a five-year-old.

For reference only.

HAROLD THORNE, 400.

Bay horse, foaled April 10, 1885.

Owned at Payne Stock Farm.

BY

HEPTAGON, 1230.

Sire of Amboy, 2:30; Cleon, 2:22; Huntsman (4), 2:30; full brother to Hermes, 2:27½; by Harold, sire of Maud S., 2:08¾, etc., by Hambletonian, 10.

Dam, PHANTOM . . . . by THORNDALE, 305, 2:22¼.

2d dam, LADY WORTH . . . . . by HAMBLETONIAN, 10.

3d dam, STEVE WURTZ, mare . . . by ABDALLAH I.

Description. — This horse is a handsome bay; star; hind feet white; 16 hands high; 1200 lbs. weight. He has three Hambletonian crosses, a Mambrino Chief cross through Dolly, the dam of Thorndale, 2:22¼; Onward, 2:25¼; and Director, 2:17; the sire of Direct, fastest pacing record 2:06. No mare living or dead ever produced three such noted sons and all by different sires. Edwin Forrest sired the dam of Mambrino King, pronounced by officers of the French government to be the handsomest horse in the world. He sired Prince Regent 2:16½; winner of the $10,000 race at Hartford in 1890; also, Nightingale, 2:18½; winner of the same stake in 1891. Edwin Forrest sired the dam of Dr. Herr (son of Mambrino Patchen), the sire of Joe Davis, 2:17¾; winner of the purse in 1885. Edwin Forrest sired the grandam of Nancy Hanks, 2:09, winner of the five-year-old stake, beating Allerton, record 2:09¼, in three straight heats in 2:12, 2:12¾, and 2:12, the fastest three heats ever trotted, and each heat being faster than any ever before trotted in a race. Harold Thorne has five lines to Abdallah I., the sire of Hambletonian 10, the founder of the greatest trotting family.

Harold Thorne made his first season in the stud when three years old, and his oldest colts are three years old in 1892. They show great promise, but like his sire, have never been trained. Harold Thorne was awarded first prize at the Bay State Fair, Boston, Mass., October, 1886; first prize at the National Horse Show, New York, November, 1886; first prize at New England Fair, Worcester, Mass., September, 1887, and at Bay State Fair, Springfield, Mass., October, 1888.

No. 56.   # BUSS THORNE.

(Standard and registered Vol. XII.)

Bay gelding, foaled May 11, 1892.

Bred at Payne Farm.

BY

HAROLD THORNE, 400.

Son of Heptagon, 1230; dam, Phantom, by Thorndale, 305.

Dam, WALKILL TELL . . . . . by WILLIAM TELL, 1602.
Vol. VI., p. 305.   By Knickerbocker, 200; dam Gossip, dam of one, by Mambrino Patchen, 58.

2d dam, WALKILL MAID . . . . by HAMBLETONIAN, 10.
Vol. X., p. 415. Sire of 40 from 2:17¼; 138 sons with 1182; 69 dams of 89 from 2:08.

3d dam, SALLY FEAGLES . . . . by SMITH'S CLAY.
Son of Cassius M. Clay, Jr.

4th dam . . . . by HICKORY.

Description. — Buss Thorne is a bay, with off fore pastern, and nigh hind ankle white, broken, and good size. He will make a fast horse. He tracks five times to Hambletonian. His grandam (Walkill Maid), like Kremlin's, 2:07¾, is by Hambletonian. She is an own sister of Dauntless, the sire of Gene Smith, 2:15½; Thornless, 2:15¾; Hendryx, 2:17½; Ed Annan, 2:16¼. He has three Clay lines, and two Mambrino Chief Strains. All this colt wants is a chance, and he will not only trot fast, but will make a race-horse. He is sound.

No. 57. DORENE.

(Standard and registered Vol. XII.)

Bay filly, foaled June 27, 1892,

Bred at Payne Farm.

BY

HAROLD THORNE, 400

Son of Heptagon, 1230; dam, Phantom, by Thorndale, 305.

Dam, DORA . . . . by THORNDALE, 305.
Vol. V., p. 178. Sire of 7 from 2:16¼; 5 speed getters; 7 dams of 15 great race horses.

2d dam, DAUNTLESS by HARRY CLAY, 45.
Sire of 4 from 2:19; 9 speed getters; 17 dams of 29.

3d dam, DOLL . . . . by CASSIUS M. CLAY, Jr. (Corning's).

4th dam, WATSON MARE . . . . by L. I. BLACK HAWK, 24.

Description.— Dorene is a bay with white between nostrils, and off hind pastern white; broken, kind, and of good size. This filly will make a large, fine mare, and is bred in speedy lines. She traces four times to Hambletonian. Her sire dam and her dam are by Thorndale, 2:22¼; the sire of Edwin Thorne, 2:16½; Daisy Dale, 2:19¼; and other fast ones. He also sired the dam of Egthorne, 2:12¼. Thorndale's dam, Dolly, is the dam of Director, 2:17, the sire of Directum, three-year-old record, 2:11¾; Evangeline (4), 2:11¾; Margaret S., 2:12½; Guide, 2:16¼; Direct, 2:05½. Dorene's grandam is by Harry Clay. He sired the dam of Electioneer, the sire of Arion, two-year-old record, 2:10¾; three-year-old record, 2:10½. Sound.

No. 58. LA TELL.

(Standard and registered Vol. XII.)

Black gelding, foaled May 23, 1892.

Bred at Payne Farm.

BY

WILLIAM TELL, 1692.

Son of Knickerbocker, 200; dam, Gossip, dam of Altus, by Mambrino Patchen, 58.

Dam, JULIA LELAND . . . . . . by LELAND, 1300.
Vol. 7, p. 411.   Sire of Geneva, 2:14; and 6 other fast ones.

2d dam, BARONESS . . . . by HARRY CLAY, 45.
Vol. V., p. 304. See Lady Vander-   Sire of 4 from 2:19; 9 speed getters;
bilt, Vol. IV., p. 345.   17 dams of 20.

3d dam, THE HARRIS MARE.
(One of a fast pair brought from Canada and known in Albany as the Harris team.)

Description.— La Tell is black with a large star, of good size, broken, kind, and very intelligent. He is finely bred, tracing twice to Hambletonian. Has three Clay lines. Has five lines to Abdallah, the sire of Hambletonian, and has three lines to Imp. Bellfounder, the sire of Hambletonian's dam. He also has a Mambrino Chief strain through Mambrino Patchen, and a Star cross. The third dam of Kremlin, 2:07¾, was by American Star. Leland, the sire of La Tell's dam, is the sire of Geneva, 2:14. Harry Clay, the sire of his grandam, is the sire of the dam of the great Electioneer, the sire of 132 trotters with records from 2:08¼ to 2:30. Sound.

No. 59. ARTHUR THORNE.

(Standard and registered Vol. XII.)

Bay gelding, foaled June 2, 1892.

Bred at Payne Farm.

BY

HAROLD THORNE, 400.

(Son of Heptagon, 1230; dam, Phantom, by Thorndale, 305.)

Dam, AMIE TELL . . . . by WILLIAM TELL, 1692.
Vol. VI., p. 194.   Son of Knickerbocker, 200; dam, Gossip (dam of one), by Mambrino Patchen, 58.

2d dam, JESSIE McCONNELL . . . by SENATOR, 277.
Vol. V., p. 210. Dam of Favorite,   Sire of Favorite, 2:30.
2:30.

3d dam, MAD PATCH . . . . . . by GEO. M. PATCHEN, 30.
    Vol. II., p. 370.   Sire of 4 from 2:18¼; 14 sons with
                  56; 4 dams of 5.

4th dam, PENELOPE . . . . . . by ABDALLAH I.
                  Sire of 3; 1 son with 40; 7 dams of
                  trotters.

5th dam . . . . by MESSENGER DUROC.
                  By Sir Duroc, he by Sir Archy, by
                  Imp. Diomed.

Description.— Arthur Thorne is a bay with a star, and off fore foot white. Large and broken. Has a splendid disposition, and will make a fine, large horse. He is bred in trotting lines to go with the best, and will have size enough for a fine family carriage horse if he does not prove a trotter. He has four lines to Hambletonian. Four Clay lines, two of them through George M. Patchen, the greatest Clay. He traces ten times to old Abdallah, the sire of Hambletonian, besides two lines to Mambrino Chief, one through Mambrino Patchen, the Chief's greatest sire, and one through Dolly, the dam of Director, 2:17, the sire of Direct, 2:05½ (pacing record). Sound.

No. 60. KALEIDOSCOPE.

Standard and registered, Vol. XII.

Bay filly, foaled May 2, 1892; bred at Payne Farm.

BY

TELESCOPE, 7500,

Son of William Tell, 1692; dam, Belle Ericsson, by Mambrino Patchen, 58.

Dam, WEST TELL . . . . by WILLIAM TELL, 1692.
    Vol. VI., p. 366.   Son of Knickerbocker, 200; dam,
                  Gossip (dam of 1), by Mambrino
                  Patchen, 58.

2d dam, WESTON GIRL . . . . . by ADMINISTRATOR, 357.
    Vol. IV., p. 290; dam of Tribune,   Sire of 13 in list; 15 sires of 26; 29
    2:25¼.   dams of 33 race horses.

3d dam, SCHOOL GIRL . . . . . by MAMBRINO PATCHEN, 58.
                  Sire of 22 trotters; 39 sons with 100;
                  65 dams of 82.

4th dam, PRECEPTRESS . . . . . by CASSIUS M. CLAY, 22.
    Vol. III., p. 523.   Sire of 4; 10 sons with 31; 26 daughters with 34.

5th dam . . . . by BERTRAND.

Description.— Kaleidoscope is a bay with elongated star, white on nose, nigh hind foot white. Broken, large, and fine. Will make a large, elegant, fast carriage mare. All her ancestors are large and fine. She has four direct lines to Mambrino Patchen. Mambrino Patchen mares are the dams of Alcyone, the sire of Martha Wilkes, 2:08, Alcantara, Guy Wilkes, 2:15¼, and Constantine, 2:12¼, and many other good ones. Telescope's dam was by Mambrino Patchen; his second dam was by Ericsson, the sire of the dam of Moquette, 2:10; his third dam was by Bob Letcher, by Medoc (the four-mile running horse), by American Eclipse, the winner over Henry in the great $20,000 race between the North and South. Sound.

No. 61.   PLUMB THORNE.

(Standard and registered Vol. XII.)

Bay colt, foaled June 12, 1892.

Bred at Payne Farm.

BY

HAROLD THORNE, 400.

By Heptagon, 1230; dam, Phanton, by Thorndale, 305.

Dam, NETTIE TELL . . . . Vol. VI. p. 326.	by WILLIAM TELL, 1602. By Knickerbocker, 200; dam, Gossip (dam of 1), by Mambrino Patchen, 58.
2d dam, NETTIE PLUMMER . . . Vol IX., p. 528.	by HAMBLETONIAN, 10. Sire of Dexter, 2:17¼; and 39 others; 138 sires of 1182; 69 dams of 89 from 2:08.
3d dam, COQUETTE . . .	by JUPITER, 46. Sire of 5; 2 speed getters; 5 dams of 6.
4th dam, SUFFOLK MAID	by HENRY. By Sir Archy.

Description.— Plumb Thorne is a bay colt with off hind heel white. He, too, is large, broken, and sound. He is so nice a colt in every way that he should be kept for a stallion. He will make a large, handsome horse. He combines the blood of Harold Thorne and William Tell, both prize winners. Harold Thorne, like Kremlin, 2:07¾, is by a son of Harold. The grandams of both are by Hambletonian. The grandam of Plumb Thorne is also by Hambletonian. He has five direct lines to Hambletonian. Two Mambrino Chief lines, one through Mambrino Patchen, the other through Dolly, the dam of Director, 2:17, the sire of Directum, 2:11¼, race record as a three-year-old. He has three Clay lines, one of which comes through old George M. Patchen, the greatest Clay. His fourth dam was Suffolk Maid who trotted against Lady Suffolk in 1838. She was by the race horse Henry, the competitor of American Eclipse in the great $20,000 race.

No. 62. BARONESS THORNE.

(Standard and registered Vol. XII.)

Bay filly, foaled May 22, 1892.

Bred at Payne Farm.

BY

HAROLD THORNE, 400.

(Son of Heptagon, 1280; dam Phantom, by Thorndale, 305.

Dam, BARONESS . . . . by HARRY CLAY, 45.
Vol. V., p. 804.   Sire of 4 from 2:19; 9 speed-getting
                                          sons; 17 dams of 29.

Harris mare a fast pole mare.

Description.— Baroness Thorne is a rosewood bay with large elongated
star extending over nose; nigh fore pastern white; nigh hind leg white and off
hind ankle white. Is broken and has a splendid disposition. Will make as nice
a mare as any gentleman could wish to own. Is large, and will go fast. Harold
Thorne, her sire, is by a son of Harold the same as Kremlin, 2:07¾, and this
filly is out of a mare by old Harry Clay, the sire of the dam of Electioneer, the
sire of 110 trotters. Sound. She combines the Hambletonian blood three times
with Clay and Mambrino Chief strains.

No. 63. DRIFT, 16290.

(Altered since being registered.)

Bay gelding, foaled July 21, 1891; bred at Payne Farm.

BY

WILLIAM TELL, 1692.

Son of Knickerbocker, 200; dam, Gossip, dam of one in 2:30, by Mambrino
Patchen, 58.

Dam, DORA . . . . by THORNDALE, 305.
Vol. V., p. 178.   Sire of 7; 5 speed getters; dams of
                                          Egthorne, 2:12½; Miss Alice, 2:17;
                                          Idavan, 2:19¼, and 12 others.

2d dam, DAUNTLESS . . . . . . by HARRY CLAY, 45.
                                          Sire of 4 from 2:19; 9 speed getters;
                                          17 daughters with 29.

3d dam, DOLL . . . . by C. M. CLAY, JR. (Corning's).

4th dam, WATSON MARE . . . . by L. I. BLACK HAWK, 24.

Description.— Drift is a bay, with star, near hind ankle white, and stands
15¾ hands high. Broken, and a very powerful gelding. Will make a great carriage horse. Has splendid feet and limbs, and will go fast. He is nicely bred.
Traces twice to Hambletonian, twice to Mambrino Chief, and has four Clay lines.
In fact, is a Clay in build, shape, and characteristics. The Clay blood combined
with Hambletonian produced George Wilkes and Electioneer. Sound.

No. 64. ELLA H.

(Standard and registered, Vol. X, p. 451.)

Roan mare, foaled May 25, 1891; bred at Payne Farm.

BY

WILLIAM TELL, 1692.

Son of Knickerbocker, 200; dam, Gossip, dam of Altus, 2:30, by Mambrino Patchen. 58.

Dam, JESSIE McCONNELL	by SENATOR, 277.
	Sire of Favorite, 2:30.
2d dam, MAD PATCH	by GEO. M. PATCHEN, 30.
	Sire of Lucy, 2:18¼, and 3 others; a speed-getting son with 12 and 14 with 66; 4 dams of 5.
3d dam, PENELOPE	by ABDALLAH I.
	Founder of the Hambletonian family.
4th dam	by MESSENGER DUROC.

Description.—Ella H. is a roan mare about 15¾ hands high; broken. She will make a nice road horse. Has a long, fine neck and a nice disposition. Any-one fancying a nice red roan will like this mare. She is stout and hardy, and will improve with driving all the time. Sound. She traces to Hambletonian, Mambrino Patchen, to Old George M. Patchen twice, and five times to Abdallah, the sire of Hambletonian. It will be hard to find a much better bred or a nicer one. Her grandam, like Stamboul's, is by George M. Patchen, and her great grandam, like his, is also by Abdallah.

No. 65. STALACTITE.

(Standard and registered, Vol. X, p. 597.)

Bay mare, foaled May 8, 1891; bred at Payne Farm.

BY

WILLIAM TELL, 1692.

Son of Knickerbocker, 200, out of a producing daughter of Mambrino Patchen, 58.

Dam, LADY STEVENS	by CHAMPION, 807.
	Sire of 8; 6 sons with 37; 6 dams of 7 heat winners.
2d dam	by LONG ISLAND.
3d dam	by BARTLETT'S TURK.
4th dam	by DEY'S MESSENGER.

Description.—Stalactite is a bay with elongated star, hind ankles white. Stands 15¾ hands high. Broken, and has a nice disposition. Shows speed, and will make a fine carriage mare. Is very strong and powerfully made. Her dam stands fully 16 hands, weighs 1250 lbs., and is a fine road horse. The champion mares have plenty of nerve and staying qualities. This mare will have size and quality. Sound.

No. 66.   LODI TELL.

(Standard and registered, Vol. X., p, 451.)

Bay mare, foaled June 10, 1890; bred at Payne Farm.

BY

WILLIAM TELL, 1692.

Dam, LODI MAID . . . . by WM. M. RYSDYK, 5703.
 Vol. VII., p. 438.   Sire of Lady Whitefoot, 2:18½; 2
                                   speed getters, and the dam of Myr-
                                   tle S., 2:28¼.
2d dam, POST MARE . . . . . . by CHAMPION, 807.
 Vol. V., p. 303.   Sire of 8; 6 sons with 37; 6 dams of
                                   7 race horses.
3d dam . . . . by CHANCE.
                                   by Chance, a son of thoroughbred
                                   Rattler.

Description.—Lodi Tell is a bay, nigh hind pastern white. Stands 16 hands
high. Broken. This is a very fine mare, and her equal in looks can hardly be
found. Anyone matching her will have the finest carriage team in New England.
Has never been handled for speed, but will go fast. Her dam was owned by
Lieutenant-Governor Weston, of Dalton, Mass., and used in his carriage team.
She stood 16¼ hands high, could out-road and out-style any horse of her size,
and could trot close to 2:40 without any handling. All the stock entered by the
Payne Stock Farm are sound. Should any unsoundness occur, it will be pointed
out at time of sale.

Consigned by J. W. Knibbs.

No. 67.   PHIL BENTON.

Seal brown gelding, foaled 1887.

Sixteen hands, 1075 pounds.

BY

MAJOR BENTON, 9109.

(Sire of Governor Benton, 2:22¼ ; and Dick, 2:26¼.)

(Son of Jim Scott, 836; dam, Lady Benton, a great producer.)

Dam . . . . by PHIL SHERIDAN, 630, 2:26½.
                                   Sire of 11; 4 speed getters and 6
                                   dams of 7 trotters.

Description.— This is a perfect road horse, sound and kind in stable and
harness; broken double and single. He is a very showy horse in harness and can
trot in 2:35. He has the Benton action, is bold and free, but very easy to drive.
This horse should beat 2:30.

Consignment of J. Malcolm Forbes, Ponkapog, Mass.

No. 68. BRIOSA.

Brown filly, foaled May 6, 1892; bred by J. Malcolm Forbes.

BY

PAWNEE, 17312.

Son of Stamboul, 5101, 2:08; dam, Minnehaha, dam of 5 in the list; 2 speed getters; dams of 11; 2d dam, Nettie Clay, by Cassius M. Clay, 22.

Dam, EDGELINE	by VICTOR VON BISMARCK, 326.
Sister to Edgemark (4), 2:16.	Sire of 27 from 2:16; 4 speed-getting sons; dams of 4.
2d dam, EDGEWATER BELLE . . .	by EDGEWATER, 12730.
Dam of Edgemark, 2:16.	Sire of 2; dams of Edgemark, 2:16; and Wilto (3), 2:29.
3d dam, EASTER	by AMERICAN CLAY, 34.
	Sire of 3; 2 speed getters; 27 dams of 32.
4th dam, NANNIE MARDENS . . .	by ERICSSON, 130.
	Sire of 6; 3 speed-getting sons; 12 dams of trotters.

Description.—Here is a royally bred filly, whose blood lines entitle her to a place on any farm in America. Look at the magnificent breeding of her sire, and note the producing qualities on the maternal side. There is enough Hambletonian 10 blood in the pedigree to almost warrant a producer of extreme speed.

No. 69. CORVA.

Brown colt, foaled May 13, 1892.

Bred by J. Malcolm Forbes.

BY

PAWNEE, 17312.

Son of Stamboul, 5101, 2:08; dam, Minnehaha, dam of 5 in the list; 2 speed getters; dams of 11; 2d dam, Nettie Clay, by Cassius M. Clay, 22.

Dam, TITANIA	by ELECTIONEER, 125.
	Sire of 120 in the list from 2:08¼; 27 sons with 108; 22 dams of 24.
2d dam, EILA	by DEL SUR, 1098; 2:24.
	Sire of 4 from 2:10¾; sire of dam of Lady II., 2:18.
3d dam, EILEEN OGE	by NORFOLK.
4th dam	by OWEN DALE.

Description.— This representative of the highest type of California breeding is a rare prize. Here is the Stamboul, Electioneer, Minnehaha combination, and through individuals selected for their excellence. Corva must make a grand stock horse and is bred for a speed phenomenon.

No. 70. CRAVO.

Bay colt, foaled April 24, 1892.

Bred by J. Malcolm Forbes.

BY

EDGEMARK (4), 7432, 2:16.

(Champion colt trotter of his age, when the mark was made.)

Dam, MAGGIE SULTAN . . . . . by SULTAN, 1513; 2:24.
Three-year-old record, 2:30.   Sire of 28 from 2:08; 6 speed getters; dams of 7 from 2:11¾.

2d dam, MAGGIE PRESCOTT . . . by JIM MONROE, 835.
Public trial, 2:23½.   Sire of 8 from 2:19; 2 speed getters; 10 dams of speed from 2:10½.

3d dam, LAURA LOGAN . . . . . by AMERICAN CLAY, 34.
Dam of St. Valentine, 2:17½;   Sire of 3; 2 speed getters; 37 dams
Judge Hawes, 2:23; Maggie   of 32.
Prescott and Lubins (2), 2:30.

4th dam, PEG . . . . by LOW'S CRUSADER.

Description.—There is trot in every line of this colt's breeding and rarely is one with such a rich inheritance put on the market. He is fashionably, stoutly, and superbly bred, and cannot fail to be a grand investment.

No. 71. PANDORAS.

Roan colt, foaled May 26, 1892.

Bred by J. Malcolm Forbes.

BY

EDGEMARK (4), 7432, 2:16.

(Champion four-year-old stallion in his day.)

Dam PANDORA . . . . by BEN FRANKLIN, 753, 2:29.
Sire of 23 from 2:20¼; a speed-getting son and the dam of Capt. Thorne (3), 2:18½.

2d dam . . . . . by DeLONG'S ETHAN ALLEN (4), 860, 243. Sire of 3 in the list; dams of 3 in the list.

3d dam . . . . by YOUNG HAWK'S EYE.

Description.—With the steady rise in the value of Lambert brood-mares, this ought to make a good investment. This class of combination gave the world a Pamlico and a Jay Bird.

47

2

67

Consignment of J. C. Otis,

No. 72.

Bay gelding, 5 years old.

Bred by M. Smith, Ionia, Mich.

BY

MONTGOMERY, 3512; 2:21¼.

By Inheritor, 1244; dam, Bazaar (dam of Fanny Wilkes, 2:26¼; and Effie, 2:27¼), by Kentucky Chief.

Dam, HANNAH . . . . by s. t. b. by son of Genknox.

Description.—Broken double and single, strip in face, ankles white, is good gaited and with handling would make a fast horse. Montgomery is sire of "Cleveland S.," 2:11¼. In addition to this he is out of a mare that has put three in the list and he is a sure sire of early speed and race horse qualities.

No. 73.

Bay gelding, 2 years old.

Bred by J. C. Otis, Norwell, Mass.

BY

AMERICAN LAD, 8842; 2:26½.

Son of Ethan Wilkes, 6417; dam, Rarity by Messenger Bashaw; 2d dam by Lexington.

Dam, JUDITH . . . . by s. t. b. MASTERLODE, 595.

Sire of 23 from 2:15¼; 12 sons with 18, and 9 dams of 10 in the list.

Description.—This colt is good size, a nice bay with faint star and snip, no other white, broken single and double. He has never been handled for speed; is well gaited enough to go along some. He will make a fine gentleman's driver, as his dam is a natural roadster of ten to twelve miles an hour on her courage and has endurance enough to do it all day.

Consignment of T. E. Scanlan.

No. 74.　　FLOWER GIRL.

Bay filly, foaled 1892; bred by T. E. Scanlan.

BY

NORWOOD, 522.

Dam, CAPER . . . . by KENTUCKY WILKES, 2:21¼.

2d dam, MASON GIRL . . . . . . by ARABIAN CHIEF.
Dam of Alroy, 2:23.

3d dam, LADY MASON . . . . . by AMERICAN STAR, 14.

4th dam . . . . by COMMODORE.

Description.— Flower Girl is bred for a trotter, and gives every promise of being one. She is of fair size, has a very clever way of going, and can show speed. She is bred well enough for anyone, and in producing lines.

No. 75.   CAPER.

Bay mare, foaled May 28, 1889.

Bred at Marchland Farm.

BY

KENTUCKY WILKES, 2:21¼.

Dam, MASON GIRL . . . . by ARABIAN CHIEF.
  Dam of Alroy, 2:23.

2d dam, LADY MASON . . . . . . by AMERICAN STAR, 14.
  Dam of a producer.

3d dam . . . . by COMMODORE.

Description.— This standard bred mare out of a producer of a great race horse and sired by a getter of speed and a horse that stood the test of campaigning, ought to make a great brood-mare. She is of good size, well made, and ought to make a trotter.

Consignment of S. C. Bailey, Ticonderoga, N. Y.

No. 76.   FRANKLINWOOD.

Bay mare; standard bred,

BY

BLACKWOOD (3), 74, 2:31.

Sire of Protoine, 2:18, and 6 others; 7 speed getters and 14 dams of 19 in list.

Dam, LADY BURNS . . . . . . by BEN FRANKLIN, 2:29.
  Four-year-old record, 2:46. Also   Sire of 23 from 2:20¼; 1 speed-
  the dam of New England   getting son and the dam of a three-
  Queen, 2:32.   year-old in 2:18½.

2d dam . . . . by THE HOWARD HORSE.
                    Son of Old Blackhawk, 5.

Description.— Bay mare stands 15 hands, 1½ inches; sound, kind, broken single and double; can show a 2:50 gait. This filly should prove to be a great brood-mare, bred as she is with Morgan and Mambrino Chief cross. Blackwood, 74, sired the dams of six new 2:30 performers last year with a total of 19 in the list. Ben Franklin brood-mares are every day proving their ability.

No. 77. DOANWOOD.

Black filly, foaled 1890.

BY

BLACKWOOD (3), 74, 2:31.

(Sire of Proteine, 2:18 and 6 others; 7 speed getters and dams of 19 in list.) By
Alexander's Norman, 25; dam, Rose Edwards by a grandson of Mambrino
Chief, 11.

Dam, DOAN MARE . . . . by COLUMBUS, 95.
 Dam of Dickard, 2:25.   Sire of 11; 6 sons with 19; 8 dams of
                9.

2d dam . . . . by VERMONT BLACK HAWK, 5.
                Sire of Ethan Allen, etc.; 14 sons
                with 23 in list; dams of Gen.
                Tweed and Tennessee.

3d dam . . . . by BISHOP'S HAMBLETONIAN.
                Sire of Hambletonian, 2, sire of 3; 1
                speed getter and the dams of 6 in
                the list.

Description. — This is a handsome black filly, 15 hands high, broken
double and single. She is nicely gaited and shows a great turn of speed. She
should make a splendid brood-mare after she has been trotted a season or two.

No. 78. MARGARET.

Brown mare, foaled 1886.

BY

DANIEL LAMBERT (3), 102, 2:42.

Sire of 36 trotters from 2:19¼; 27 sons with 81 in the list and 29 daughters with
40.

Dam, CALKINS MARE . . . . . by BIGELOW HORSE.
 Half sister to the dam of Frank,   Son of Black Hawk, 5, sire of the
  2:19¼; 2:08 to pole.   dam of Haldome, 2:26, sire of Halo,
                etc,

Description. — Brown; 16 hands high; nigh hind ankle white. Bred by
Samuel Root, Westport, N. Y.; has been used exclusively for road purposes until
put to breeding. One of her foals is sure to enter the 2:30 list this season. Bred
to Victor Wilkes, Sept. 12.

No. 79.   VERMONT.

Bay horse, foaled 1890.

BY

VERMONT VOLUNTEER.

Dam . . . . by GEN'L SHERMAN, 862.
> Record 2:38; sire of 4 in list; a speed-getting son, and the dams of 2.

2d dam . . . . by THE HOWARD HORSE.
> Son of Old Black Hawk.

Description.— Bay; 15¼ hands high; broken single and double; safe for lady to drive; can show considerable speed and will make a very nice family horse.

No. 80.   HATTO.

Bay mare; bred by H. Y. Simpson, Worcester, Mass.; standard and registered,

BY

THORNDALE, 305, 2: 22¼.

Sire of Edwin Thorn, 2:16¼, and 6 others; 5 speed getters; dams of Miss Alice, Idavan, Dr. West, Watchword, and 10 others.

Dam, GOSSIP . . . . by HARRY CLAY, 45; 2:29.
> Sire of Clayton, 2:19, etc.; 9 sires of 15 and 17 dams of 20.

2d dam, GERTRUDE . . . . by IMP. LAPIDIST, 4451.

3d dam, LADY MAXON . . . . . by IMP. CONSTERNATION, 3441.

4th dam, LADY CLINTON . . . . by REVOLUTION, 2052.

5th dam, YOUNG MOGG . . . . . by BILLY W. DUROC.

6th dam, OLD MOGG.
Thoroughbred.

Description.— Bay mare; 15 hands, 1½ inches high; broken both single and double. She has a pacing record of 2:44. She was bred to Hyperion in '92, and is a regular breeder, and has proven herself a good brood-mare. She is safe for a lady to drive. She is the dam of one colt sold to A. E. Tainter of New York, for $2,500 at a year old. Look at the royalty of her breeding for those who want grand thoroughbred backing.

No. 81.   MAJOR.

Bay gelding, foaled May 10, 1891.

Bred by J. B. Haggin, El Paso, Cal.

BY

ALBERT W., 2:20.

Sire of Little Albert, 2:10¼; Flowing Tide, 2:14¾, etc., etc.

Dam, PIRATE QUEEN	by BUCCANEER, 2656. Son of Iowa Chief, 528; and sire of Flight, 2:20; Shamrock (2), 2:25, etc., etc.
2d dam, ECHO QUEEN.	by YOUNG ECHO. Son of Echo, 462, out of Huntress, 2:24; dam of Hidalgo, 2:27.
3d dam, QUEEN OF HEARTS . . .	by SAMPSON, 276. Son of Hambletonian, 10.
4th dam, LADY CRAWFORD . . .	by AMERICAN STAR, 14.
5th dam, OLD LADY	by HECTOR. Son of Latourette's Bellfounder.

Description.—Bay 15¼ hands; foaled May 10, 1891; bred by J. B. Haggin, Rancho Del Paso Farm, California. Small white mark in forehead, snip on nose; near forefoot white, off fore leg white above the pastern; branded 41 under mane; broken double and single; kind, good disposition; should trot fast if trained. This is a great bred youngster; should develop into a fast one; he is from a first-class producing family.

No. 82.   BELLE OF PUTNAM.

Brown mare, foaled 1888.

BY

LAMBERT CHIEF.

Son of Daniel Lambert.

Dam	. . . . . . by GOURLEY HORSE. Son of C. W. Mitchell; sire of Helping Hand, 2:28, etc., etc.

Description.—Brown, 16 hands high; bred by Thomas Maxwell, Putnam, N. Y. Broken single and double; splendid roadster; should trot fast if trained; she is from a speed-producing family.

No. 83.   LIZZIE H.

Bay mare; foaled 1890.

BY

BENEFIT, 5327.

Son of General Benton, sire of Sallie Benton, 2:17½; the Seer, 2:19½; Lord Byron, 2:18, etc.; dams of Sunol, 2:08¼, etc., etc.

Dam, GAZELLE . . . . by PRIMERS, 2:55.
     Dam of Fowler boy, 2:29½.   Son of Marshall Chief, 452, out of a daughter of Young Messenger.

2d dam, MAYFLY, 2:30¼ . . . . . by ST. CLAIR, 16075.
     Dam of Bonita (4), 2:18½; Mecca,   Sire of dams of Manzanita (4), 2:16;
     Gazelle, etc.   Bonita (4), 2:18½; Wildflower (2), 2:21; Fred Crocker (2), 2:25¼.

Description. — This mare is branded J. 147, and was bred by Hon. Leland Stanford. She is broken single and double, is an elegant roadster, and is clever to saddle. A child has used her. Her breeding entitles her to be a great producer.

No. 84.   DANDY.

Bay gelding, foaled 1886.

Breeding unknown. Bred in Kentucky and is about ⅞ thoroughbred.

Description. — Bay, 15½ hands high; broken single and double; cheerful, pleasant driver, and one of the finest saddle horses in the country. Should make a great all around horse for any gentleman.

No. 85.   BONEY.

Bay horse; bred by John Root, Benson, Vt.

BY

BONIFIED. (I. V. BAKER'S HORSE.)

Dam . . . . by BAY LAMBERT.

2d dam . . . . by THE HOWARD HORSE.
     He by Old Black Hawk.

Description. — Bay stands 15½ hands; very stylish, great knee actor; broken single and double, and can show a great deal of speed. If handled should make a fast horse. Foaled in 1890.

No. 86.
MYRON.
Sorrel horse, foaled 1886.

One of pair.

BY

ARISTOS, 271, 2:27¾.

Sire of 14; 5 speed getters and dams of 3.

Dam . . . . by BAY COLUMBUS.
2d dam . . . . by SHERMAN'S BLACK HAWK.

Description.— Sorrel horse, 16¼ hands high, two white ankles behind; foaled in 1886; sired by Aristos (2:27), out of the dam of Toby by Daniel Lambert (2:32). Broken single and double, perfectly sound, kind, safe for a lady to drive; and can show a three-minute gait single.

No. 87.
DANDY.
Sorrel horse, foaled 1887.

One of pair.

BY

BOSAR.

By Hambletonian.

Dam . . . . by BAY LAMBERT.
Son of Daniel Lambert.
2d dam . . . . by OLD COLUMBUS.

Description.—Sorrel horse, two white ankles and white face. Foaled in 1887; broken single and double, perfectly sound, and kind, and fearless every way. Can show a three-minute gait single.

No. 88.
RUTH.
Bay mare, foaled 1889.

BY

BLACKWOOD (3), 74, 2:26.

(Sire of Proteine, 2:18; and 6 others; 7 speed getters and dams of 19 in list.)

By Alexander's Norman, 25; dam, Rose Edwards, by grandson of Mambrino Chief, 11.

Dam, ALPEAN . . . . by MONTELLO, 1900.
2d dam, THE DOAN MARE . . . . by COLUMBUS, 95.
Dam of Dickard (2:25). Sire of 11; 6 speed-getting sons and dams of 9.

3d dam . . . . by BLACK HAWK, 5.

Sire of 4; 14 sons with 23; dams of 20.

4th dam . . . . by BISHOP'S HAMBLETONIAN.

Description.—Bay mare, stands 15 hands 1½ inches; broken single and double, is a little inclined to pace. Foaled in 1889, showed a mile in 2:50 as a two-year-old over the ice. She won second money in the two-year-old race on Lake George. She was bred the next year (1892), but did not prove with foal. This is a very promising filly and from her breeding and her individuality should make a race horse.

No. 89.　　　ALPEAN.

Chestnut mare, standard and registered; foaled 1886.

BY

MONTELLO, 1900.

Dam, DOAN MARE . . . . by BAY COLUMBUS, 95.
　Dam of Dickard, 2:25.　　　　Sire of 11; 6 speed-getting sons and dams of 9.

2d dam . . . . by OLD BLACK HAWK.

Sire of 4; 14 sons with 23; dams of 20.

3d dam . . . . by BISHOP'S HAMBLETONIAN.

Description.— Fifteen ¼ hands; broken single and double; never has been worked any for speed; has been in the stud since she was two years old; should make a very fast mare if trained, and was stinted to a son of Guy Wilkes last year.

Consignment of J. W. Matthewson.

No. 90.　　　SPONSOR, 11712.

Bay colt, foaled March 29, 1889.

Bred by M. L. Hare, Indianapolis.

BY

HAMBRINO, 820, 2:21¼.

Sire of Delmarch, 2:11½; and 19 others; 4 great speed getters; 9 dams of 12 including one dam of 2 and one of 3 in the list.

Dam, FASHION . . . . by CURTIS HAMBLETONIAN, 589.
　Dam of Pomona, 2:25; Gladstone,　　Sire of 4 in the list; 4 speed-getting
　2:28¼; Belle Ure, 2:29¾;　　　sons; and dams of 4.

3d dam, PICCOLI . . . . by MAMBRINO CHIEF, 11.
Sire of 6 from 2:18¼; 23 sires of 02;
17 dams of 24.

3d dam . . . . by OLD GREY EAGLE.

Description.—Sponsor is a natural trotter and one of the handsomest stallions ever raised. He is full brother to Pomona, 2:25; Gladstone, 2:28¼; Belle Ure, 2:28¼. You will see by his breeding he combines the blood of Hambletonian and Mambrino Chief with his dam Fashion. In the great brood-mare list he should make a sire of race horses of the highest order. Sponsor has never been worked for speed, but with the pure trotting action he possesses and his elegant bloodlines, he will beat '30 with very little handling. He is a colt of magnificent conformation, well coupled, good bone and great style.

Hambrino is everywhere known and acknowledged to be a most prepotent sire of speed and stamina. He has 24 in the 2:30 list; including Delmarch, 2:11¼; has 4 sons that have sired 22 2:30 performers; has 6 daughters that are the dams of 8 2:30 performers, two of them being great brood-mares. Hambrino will this season far surpass all he has ever done.

No. 91.   SETH CLOVER.

Gelding colt, foaled July 31, 1887.

Bred by G. C. Dempsey, Springboro, Pa.

BY

BIGAROON.

Sire of Bigaroon, Jr., Florence J., Bertha, Pete Reed, Begota, Terry Barton, and other money-earners. (Son of Imp. Bonnie Scotland; dam, Laura Bruce, the great four-miler, through which mare he is inbred.)

Dam, BELLE D. . . : . . . . . . by BELMONT.
   Sold to Governor Stafford for   Sire of Irene, Bomessia, Blossly,
   $7,500.   etc. (son of Lexington)· dam by a
           son of Boston.

2d dam, INFALLIBLE . . . . . . by LIGHTNING.
   Dam of Belle D.   Son of Lexington.

3d dam, LAURA BRUCE . . . . . by STAR DAVIS.

4th dam, ALIDA . . . . by BUFORD.

5th dam, SARPUSETTE . . . . . by IMP. SARPEDON.

6th dam, SUSETTE . . . . by ARATUS.

7th dam, JENNIE COCKRACY . . . by POTOMAC.

8th dam . . . . by IMP. SALTRAM.

Description.—Bigaroon met, as a four-year-old, such good ones as Nelly Bush, Romance, Regent, Spendrift, Molly Cad, Lady Ida, Belle Mahone, Boaster, Jim Conner, Bob Craig, Sabina, and the great Morlachi, and defeated them with perfect ease, stamping him as one of Bonnie's best sons.

Consignment of Z. E. Simmons, Lexington, Ky.

No. 92.   PRINCE SIMMONS, 20559.

Br. c., foaled 1892; bred at Wilkes Lodge.

BY

SIMMONS, 2744, 2:28.

Sire of Greenleaf, 2:10½; New York Central, 2:18¼; Coralloid, 2:14¾, and 26 other race horses; 3 speed getters; only 14 years old; son of George Wilkes; dam, Black Jane, dam of Rosa, 2:18¼, by Mambrino Patchen, 58.

Dam, PRINCESS RENE . . . . . by KING RENE, 1278, 2:30¼.
Sire of Sarcanett, 2:16¼, and 21 others; 8 sires of 10, and 5 dams of 7 heat winners.

2d dam, POLLY PATCHEN . . . . by MAMBRINO PATCHEN, 58.
Sire of 22; 39 sons with 100; 65 dams of 82 from 2:09¾.

3d dam, MARIA BARNES . . . . by RYLAND, 3580.
Sire of Blanche Clemons, 2:27¼.

4th dam . . . . by HOWARD'S ABDALLAH.
Son of Abdallah, 15.

Description.— This is a fine looking colt, and is bred to go fast. He has not been broken, but shows great speed in the lot, and is good gaited. He has the best kind of a disposition.

No. 93.   KATY F.

Bay filly, foaled June 26, 1892; bred by Z. E. Simmons, Wilkes Lodge.

BY

FLORIDA, 482.

Sire of 4 in 2:20; 12 trotters in 2:30; 7 sons that have bred on and sired speed.

Dam, KATY K. . . . . by GEORGE WILKES, 519, 2:22.
Sire of 78; 13 in 2:20; 83 sons with 792; 51 dams of 65 from 2:11¼.

2d dam . . . . by LEXINGTON.
Sire of the dams of 4; 3 speed getters; dams of 3 getters of 15; dams of the producers of Jay-Eye-See, Sunol, and 8 others.

Description.— This is a handsome bay filly, with near hind pastern white. That she shows a grand and speedy way of going cannot be wondered at from her breeding. Fillies out of George Wilkes mares are too good goods to need praise, especially when by such a horse as Florida.

No. 94. BONNIE.

Ch. f., foaled May 4, 1892; bred by Z. E. Simmons, Wilkes Lodge.

BY

BONNIE McGREGOR, 3778; 2:13½.

Sire of Ethel B., 2:19¼; Adelaide McGregor (2), 2:20¼; Bonnie Mack, 2:20¼, and Burt, 2:20¼.

Dam, NELLIE WILKES	by ABDALLAH WILKES, 7562.
Half sister to Navarro, 2:26¼.	Sire of Saxon, 2:22½, and Voleta, 2:26¾.
2d dam, NELLY G.	by ELECTIONEER, 125.
Dam of Navarro, 2:26¼.	Sire of 120 in the list; 27 sons with 106; 22 daughters with 24.
3d dam	by PRINCE OF ORANGE.
	Son of Hambletonian, 157.
4th dam	by MAMBRINO PAYMASTER.

Description.— This filly has a strip in face with hind ankles white, and is a sure trotter. She combines the blood of Robert McGregor, George Wilkes, and Electioneer, backed up by the brood-mare elements of the Mambrinos. It is producing lines, also, and her second dam was the dam of Navarro.

No. 95. AMY G.

Bay filly, foaled April 30, 1892; bred by Z. E. Simmons, Wilkes Lodge.

BY

ALFRED G., 12452, 2:19¾.

Son of Anteeo, 7868; dam, Rosa B, Speculation, 928.

Dam, FEDIE	by FERGUSON, 8015.
	Sire of 8 from 2:11½; son of George Wilkes; dam, the dam of Favorita, 2:25½.
2d dam, FIDORA	s. t. b. by HAMBLETONIAN, 10.
	Sire of 40; 138 sons with 1182; 69 dams of 89.
3d dam	s. t. b. by BATHGATE'S NORMAN.

Description.—This filly has a star and nigh hind pastern white. She is good gaited, has an excellent disposition, and though not broken shows an excellent way of going. Here is the blood of Electioneer and George Wilkes through two great lines.

No. 96. FLOBERT.

Bay colt, foaled July 18, 1892; bred at Wilkes Lodge.

BY

FLORIDA, 482.

Sire of 4 in 2:20; 12 in 2:30; 7 sires of speed.

Dam, HATTIE D. . . . . by WOODWARD'S ETHAN.
Son of Ethan Allen.

2d dam, MAGGIE . . . . by DANIEL LAMBERT, 102.
Sire of 36; 27 sires of 81; 29 dams of 40.

3d dam . . . . by WALKILL CHIEF, 330.
Sire of 2 in 2:18; 5 in 2:30; 9 sires of 12; 5 dams of 5.

Description.— This colt is a bay with hind pasterns white, and is as finely gaited as any ever bred at Wilkes Lodge. He is a natural trotter, and goes as if, when broken, he would make a race horse.

No. 97. WONDA.

Bay filly, foaled April 6, 1892; bred by Z. E. Simmons.

BY

WILLIAM L., 4244.

Sire of Axtell, 2:12 at 3 years; Emperor Wilkes, 2:20¾, and Alexis, 2:18; 1 sire of 2 colt trotters, and the dam of Winks, 2:28½.

Dam, LIZZIE TREACEY . . . . . by GEORGE WILKES, 519, 2:22.
Sister to Nelly L., 2:23¼.
Sire of 78; 13 in 20; 83 sons with 792; 51 dams of 65 from 2:11½.

2d dam, LADY OAKS . . . . . . by GILL'S VERMONT, 104.
Dam of Nelly L., 2:23¼.
Sire of Bonner Boy, 2:23; 1 speed getter; 10 dams of 12.

3d dam, KATE HUNTER . . . . . by KINCAID'S St. LAWRENCE.

4th dam, BRENDA . . . . by THOROUGHBRED.

Description.—This is a bay filly, with white face and near hind pastern white. She is broken, and shows an excellent way of going, and speed. She is an inbred Wilkes, and ought to be a fast trotter.

Consignment of Albion Towle.

No. 98.   **ZENOBIA.**

Ch. m., foaled 1885; full sister to El Capitan, 2:20¼.

BY

ALCANTARA (4), 729, 2:23.

Sire of 51 from 2:12¼; 12 sons with 17 in the list; 5 dams of 7 great race horses.

Dam, PIEDMONT MAID	by PIEDMONT, 904, 2:17¼.
Dam of El Capitan, 2:20¼.	Sire of 13 from 2:18¼; a speed getter, and 5 dams of 7.
2d dam, MINNEHAHA .`	by HAMBLETONIAN, 10.
	Sire of 40 from 2:17¼; 138 sons with 1182; 60 dams of 87 in the list.
3d dam	by BELLFOUNDER.

Description.— This full sister to the fast young horse and sire of early speed, El Capitan, is a good one. She is fine, showy, and her breeding warrants her to be fast and a producer of extreme speed. She has never been handled, but shows great speed to halter. She has been bred to the great Ralph Wilkes, 2:18, at two years old, and the result ought to make a champion.

No. 99.   **ETTA WILKES.**

Chestnut mare, foaled 1883.

Bred by J. P. McCann, Lexington, Ky.

BY

RED WILKES (4), 1749, 2:40.

Sire of 79 from 2:11¼; 18 sires of 30, and 13 mares that have produced 16.

Dam, LIZZIE	by HARRODSBURG BOY.
Dam of Etta Wilkes, 2:27¾ and Red Mack, 2:27¾.	Sire of a great producer, of the dam of Donald McKay and Pansy Blossom.
2d dam, MOLLY BERRY	by BOURBON CHIEF, 383.
Dam of a great brood-mare.	Sire of Calmar, 2:22; one speed getter and the dams of 7.
3d dam	by VERMONT, 104.
	Sire of 1; 1 speed getter; 10 dams of 12.
4th dam	s. t. b. by GREY EAGLE (Boner's).

Description.— Here is a prize and a race mare of more than ordinary merit. She was out in 1892 and every one has a chance to know that she was a game and speedy trotter. Her breeding is of the kind that produces bread winners and such a mare is cheap at any money. The owner prefers to leave her to the buyers, and expects that such a good one will be looked over by men of judgment and means.

No. 100. J. ALBA, 2:34¾.

Black horse, foaled 1887.

Owned by Albion Towle.

BY

GLEN KNOX.

Son of Howe's Bismark.

A trotting-bred mare brought from Kentucky whose pedigree has not been traced.

Description. — This horse stands 16 hands and weighs 1050 pounds; pure gaited and kind disposition. He has the best of limbs, flat and cordy — perfectly smooth without a pimple on him. He was tracked but a short time last season, and was timed separately in 2:27¼. With proper handling can trot this season in 2:20. He is second to no gentleman's horse.

Consignment of Col. H. S. Russell.

No. 101. SCOTT.

Bay gelding, foaled March 4, 1891.

Bred by H. S. Russell, Milton, Mass.

BY

EDGEMARK (4), 7432, 2:16.

(Champion colt trotter of his day; started in 11 races and never yet has been beaten.)

Dam, SMUGGLER GIRL . . . . . by SMUGGLER, 2:15¼; 927.
Sire of Mount Morris, 2:19¼; and 8 others; 10 speed-getting sons and the dams of 10 trotters.

2d dam, MADAM POWELL . . . . by BAY CHIEF.
Dam of Monroe Chief, 2:18¼; sire of 3 in the-list; 5 dams of 8 trotters including 1 dam of 3 from 2:11¼.
Sire of dams of 2 from 2:18¼; 2 speed getters; dams of the sire of a great brood-mare with 3 from 2:11¼.

3d dam . . . . by TORONTO.
Son of St. Lawrence.

Description. — Here is a representative of royal breeding. His sire was a champion and his dam was by a champion race horse. His second dam was a great producer and Scott should make a high class race trotter.

No. 102.   HARMONY.

(Dam of Puritan, 2:25 in 8th heat.)

Bay mare, foaled 1876.

Property of H. S. Russell, Milton, Mass.

BY

SMUGGLER, 927, 2:15¼.

Sire of Mount Morris, 2:10¼; and 8 others; 10 speed-getting sons and the dams
of 10 trotters.

Dam, SILKSTONE . . . . by IMP. LAPIDIST.
Son of Touchstone, dam, Io, by
Tarsus. (See A. S. B., p. 32, Vol. I.)

2d dam, PAULINE . . . . by STAR DAVIS.
Son of Imp. Glencoe; dam, Margaret
Wood, by Imp. Priam. (See Am.
Stud Book, p. 20, Vol. II.)

Description.— This mare, which is the dam of a game and fast race horse,
must prove of great value to any stock horse owner who wishes to get race horses.
She has been bred to Edgemark and the produce must be good.

No. 103.   SALVO.

Chestnut gelding, foaled May 29, 1891.

Bred by H. S. Russell, Milton, Mass.

BY

EDGEMARK (4), 7432, 2:16.

(Champion of his age when the record was made; the unbeaten hero of his colt
races.)

Dam, HARMONY . . . . by SMUGGLER, 927, 2:15¼.
Dam of Puritan, 2:25 in 8th heat.   Sire of 9 from 2:19¼; 10 speed getters
and 10 speed producers.

2d dam, SILKSTONE. . . . . . . by IMP. LAPIDIST.
Son of Touchstone, dam, Io, by
Tarsus. (See A. S. B., p. 32, Vol. I.)

3d dam, PAULINE . . . . by STAR DAVIS.
Son of Imp. Glencoe; dam, Margaret
Wood, by Imp. Priam. (See Am.
Stud Book, p. 20, Vol. II.)

Description.—Here is a ready-made race winner out of a speed producer and
by a tried race horse. He is just at the age to start work on and ought to be a
splendid investment.

No. 104.   OLIVE.

Brown mare, foaled 1883.

Bred by H. S. Russell, Milton, Mass.

BY

WEDGEWOOD, 692, 2:19.

Sire of 3 in 2:20; 16 in the list ; 4 speed-getting sons, and the dams of 5 from 2.13.

Dam, MISS LORING . . . . by SMUGGLER, 927; 2:15¼.
                                  Sire of 9 from 2:19¼ ; 10 speed getters and 10 speed producers.

2d dam, WHITE MARE . . . . . . by DONCASTER,
                                  By Trotting Childers, a son of Vermont Black Hawk, 5.

Description.— This mare is broken to harness, and has a good disposition. She is bred in producing lines and has been served by Edgemark. Her produce will be bred in the lines of three grand race horses. She stands 15¼ hands, weighs 950 pounds, and is a good individual.

No. 105.   REMUS.

Bay gelding, foaled March 11, 1890.

Bred by H. S. Russell, Milton, Mass.

BY

EDGEMARK (4)   432, 2:16.

(Champion and unbeaten colt trotter of his day.)

Dam, NETTIE T.. . . . . by SMUGGLER, 927; 2:15¼.
                                  Sire of 9 from 219¼ ; 10 speed getters and 10 producers.

2d dam, PERFECTION .   . . . by PERFECTION.

3d dam . . .   . by TORONTO.
                                  Son of St. Lawrence.

Description.— This colt should make a fast and good race horse. He is bred in lines that cannot fail to produce gameness and speed.

No. 106. # ROSE OF ERIN.

B. m., foaled 1888.

Property of II. S. Russell, Milton, Mass.

BY

SHAMROCK (2), 1510, 2:25.

Son of Buccaneer, 2650; dam, Fern Leaf, 2:40; dam of Gold Leaf, 2:11¼; by Flaxtail, 8132.

Dam, OAK GROVE BELLE . . . . by ARTHURTON, 365.
Sire of Arab, 2:15, and 4 others; 1 speed getter; 13 dams of 18 from 2:14¼.

2d dam, HENRIETTA . . . . by BELL ALTA.

No. 107. # TORY.

Bay colt; foaled April 14, 1892.

Bred by II. S. Russell, Milton, Mass.

BY

EDGEMARK (4), 7432, 2:16.

(Champion colt trotter of his age in his day.)

Dam, ROSE OF ERIN . . . . . . by SHAMROCK, (2), 12510, 2:25.
A famous colt trotter out of the dam of famous young race horses. Son of Buccaneer, 2656; dam Fern Leaf 2:40; dam of Gold Leaf, 2:11¼; by Flaxtail, 81320.

2d dam, OAK GROVE BELLE . . . by ARTHURTON, 365.
Sire of 5 from 2:15; 1 speed getter; 13 dams of 18 from 2:14¼.

3d dam, HENRIETTA . . . . . . by BELL ALTA.

Description. — This colt's wonderfully grand breeding should ensure him a royal individuality in speed and race winning ability. He is by an unbeaten colt trotter, out of a mare by a famous colt trotter, and she out of a mare by that great brood-mare sire, Arthurton. This youngster must prove a valuable investment.

No. 108.   TUSSLE.

Bay filly; foaled May 10, 1892.

Bred by H. S. Russell, Milton, Mass.

BY

EDGEMARK (4), 7432, 2:16.

(Champion and unbeaten colt trotter of his day.)

Dam, MAGENTA . . . . by MAGIC, 1451, 2:33.
                                  Sire of Clemmie G., 2:15½, and 3
                                  others; 2 speed getters and 6 dams
                                  of 11, 3 in 2:20.

2d dam, STAR QUEEN . . . . . by WHIPPLE, 8975.
                                  Sire of Glaucus and Retta; sire of
                                  dam of Chesterfield, 2:17.

Description. — This stoutly bred filly should make a great producer. She is from blood lines that have given some game, resolute and fast campaigners. Magic, backing up the great Victor Von Bismarck, with a reinforcement of the Hambletonian blood through Whipple, is too good to need comment.

No. 109.   TOMBOY.

Bay filly, foaled Feb. 27, 1892.

•   Bred by H. S. Russell, Milton, Mass.

BY

EDGEMARK (4), 7432, 2:16.

(Champion and unbeaten colt trotter of his day.)

Dam, RENA SIMMONS . . . . . by SIMMONS, 2744, 2:28.
    Sister to Col. Simmons, 2:22¾.   Sire of 5 in 2:20 from 2:10½; 29 in
                                  the list, and 3 speed getters at 13
                                  years old.

2d dam, LENA . . . . by CLARK CHIEF, JR., 3002, 2:32¼.
                                  Sire of 4 from 2:19½; 1 speed getter;
                                  and the dams of 2 young phenom-
                                  ena.

3d dam, ALICE . . . . by DOWNING'S BAY MESSENGER.

Description.— No filly living has any finer breeding than this. Her dam is a daughter of that grandson of George Wilkes which sired such race horses as Greenleaf, the only horse that won a race over Martha Wilkes in 1892. Tabulate this pedigree and see the royalty of the blood lines.

No. 110.   THEODORA.

Bay filly, foaled May 8, 1892.

Bred by H. S. Russell, Milton, Mass.

BY

EDGEMARK (4), 7432, 2:16.

(Unbeaten colt trotter of his age in his day.)

Dam, GURGLE . . . . Record, 2:20.	by POCAHONTAS BOY, 1790, 2:31. Sire of 13 from 2:12½, including that great race mare, Buffalo Girl.
2d dam, MATLOCK . . . . Dam of Sancho, 2:24¼; Gurgle, 2:20.	by GREY DIOMED. Sire of a producer of 2 in the list.
3d dam	by TOM HAL, 3000. Sire of 2 from 2:18½; dams of 3 in 2:20; 7 in 2:30.

Description.— Here is a representative of extreme speed. Her dam was a fast mare and her second dam the producer of two in the list through those stout old lines that have given the track some of its brightest lights.

No. 111.   REFORM.

Bay filly, foaled May 3, 1890.

Bred by H. S. Russell, Milton, Mass.

BY

EDGEMARK (4), 7432, 2:16.

Son of Victor Von Bismarck, sire of 27 in list; 3 speed getters; dams of 4; dam, Edgewater Belle, by Edgewater, 12730.

Dam, EMILY R.	by PEACEMAKER, 260. Sire of 2 in 2:20; 5 in 2:30; dams of 3 from 2:18¾.
2d dam, JENNY LIND	by HOAGLAND'S GREY MESSENGER, 155, 2:43; sire of 2 in list; 2 speed getters; dam of 1 —.
3d dam, JENNY LIND	by ABDALLAH, 1. Sire of 3; 1 son with 40; dams of Goldsmith Maid, and 6 others.
4th dam	by IMP. TRUSTEE.

No. 1 1 2.   SUNBEAM.

Bay filly, foaled June 9, 1891.

Bred by H. S. Russell, Milton, Mass.

(Full sister to Reform, No. 46.)

No. 1 1 3.   LAURA WILSON.

(With filly at side by Edgemark, foaled March 12, 1893, stinted again to Edgemark.) Bay mare, foaled 1880.

Property of H. S. Russell, Milton, ..Iass.

BY

SMUGGLER, 927, 2:15¼.

(Sire of 9 from 2:19¼; 10 speed getters and 10 speed producers.)

Dam, BECK . . . . by WHITE OAK.
Son of Black Hawk, 5; dam, Susie,
by Brown Davy Crockett.

2d dam . . . . by WOODFORD'S VALENTINE,
Son of Redman's Valentine, by Imp.
Valentine.

Description.— This mare should be a great producer, for being individually good, she has that stout breeding which has for a foundation the blood of
Smuggler, and carries the lines of Vermont Black Hawk, backed up by good thor-
ough breeding; she is the dam of one in the 2:30 list.

No. 1 1 4.   TALISMAN.

Bay colt; foaled Feb. 24, 1892.

Bred by H. S. Russell, Milton, Mass.

BY

EDGEMARK (4), 7432, 2:16.

(Champion colt of his day and age.)

Dam, LAURA WILSON . . . . . by SMUGGLER, 927; 2:15¼.
Dam of Kate Hamilton, 2:30.   Sire of 9 from 2:19¼; 10 speed
getters and 10 producers.

2d dam, BECK .   . . . by WHITE OAK.
Son of Black Hawk, 5; dam, Susie,
by Brown Davy Crockett.

3d dam . . . . by WOODFORD'S VALENTINE.
Son of Redman's Valentine, by Imp.
Valentine.

Description. — Here is a colt by Edgemark out of the dam of one in the
list. His individuality is good and his stout breeding guarantees a trotter.

No. 115. LAURA GIDEON.

(With foal at foot, of March 7, 1893, by Edgemark; bred back March 15.)

Grey mare; foaled, 1885.

Property of H. S. Russell, Milton, Mass.

BY

GIDEON, 145.

Dam . . . . by DANVILE BAY.

Sire of 3; 2 speed-getting sons; dams of Nelson, 2:10; Glenarm, Independence, Edna, Daisy Rolfe, Grace, and 5 others.

Description. — This mare is by the horse that sired that grand trotter, Nelson. The quality of her foals is shown by that at her side and she has been bred back to Edgemark.

No. 116. GURGLE, 2:20.

B. m., foaled 1888.

(Served by Edgemark March 17, 1893.)

BY

POCAHONTAS BOY, 1790.

Sire of 13 from 2:12½; 5 speed getters and 6 dams of 8.

Dam, MATLOCK . . . . by GREY DIOMED
Dam of 1 in 2:20.   Sire of the dam of Gurgle.

2d dam . . . . by TOM HAL, ALLISON'S.

Description. — Here is a mare that has proven herself fast and has a right to produce speed. She has a representative in the sale and is herself able to show. She was served to Edgemark, and the produce ought to be good.

No. 117. RANSOM.

B. f., foaled April 24, 1890.

Bred by H. S. Russell.

BY

EDGEMARK (4), 7432, 2:16.

Dam, GURGLE . . . . by POCAHONTAS BOY, 1790.
Record, 2:20.   Sire of 13 from 2:12½; 5 speed getters and 6 dams of 8.

2d dam, MATLOCK . . . . by GREY DIOMED.
    Dam of Gurgle, 2:20.   Sire of the dam of 1 in 2:20.

3d dam . . . . by TOM HAL.

Description. — This filly is fast and trotted a quarter last year in 38½ seconds. She is entered in the Connecticut $15,000 purse to be trotted at Hartford in 1894.

No. 118. TALLY HO.

B. c., foaled Apr. 2, 1892; bred by H. S. Russell.

BY

EDGEMARK (4), 7432, 2:16.

Unbeaten colt trotter of his day; champion record holder of his age, when made.

Dam, STAR OF HOPE . . . . . . by SHAMROCK, 12510.
                        2:25 at two years; out of the dam of
                        Gold Leaf.

2d dam, LADY BRAY . . . . . . by s. t. b. OWEN DALE.
                        Son of California Belmont.

Description. — This colt is of fair size and is broken double and single. He is gaited like Edgemark, and bred through bloodlines that have produced phenomenal early speed; should be a prize.

No. 119. ROMULUS.

B. g., foaled Feb. 13, 1890; bred by H. S. Russell.

BY

EDGEMARK (4), 7432, 2:16.

Champion four-year-old of his day.

Dam, SMUGGLER GIRL . . . . . by SMUGGLER, 927, 2:15¼.
    Dam of Amurath, 2:28.   Sire of 9 from 2:19½; 10 sires of
                        speed, and 9 producing daughters.

2d dam, MADAM POWELL . . . . by BAY CHIEF.
    Dam of Monroe Chief, 2:18¼.   Son of Mambrino Chief.

3d dam . . . . by TORONTO.
                        Son of St. Lawrence.

Description. — Romulus is of fair size, and is broken double and single. He can pace very fast. Smuggler girl is dam of Amurath, 2:28; Romulus paced a quarter in 35 seconds last year. Here is a strong bred pacer to make a money earner.

No. 120. TILLY.

B. f., foaled April 12, 1892; bred by H. S. Russell.

BY

EDGEMARK (4), 7432, 2:16.

Speed champion and race winner of his age.

Dam, MINNIE CORBITT . . . . . by GUY WILKES, 2867, 2:15¼.
  Out of a fast mare in 2:20½.   Sire of 10 in 2:20; 26 in 2:30; 3 speed
                                     getters; dam a producer.

2d dam, CARRIE T. . . . . by SIGNAL, 3327.
  Record 2:20¼.   Sire of 3; 2 in 2:20; dams of Anteeo,
                                     Jr., Nevada, and Fred Ackerman.

Description.—Tilly is of fair size. She is not very promising, but time may help her, and her breeding warrants the assumption.

No. 121. TURENNE.

Bay colt, foaled Feb. 23, 1892.

Bred by H. S. Russell.

BY

EDGEMARK (4), 7432, 2:16.

(Champion colt trotter of his age in his day.)

Dam, GRACE . . . . by BLUE BULL, 75.
                                     Sire of 59; 6 in 2:20; 31 sons with
                                     59; 43 dams of 52.

2d dam, MOLLIE D. . . . . by MAMBRINO CHIEF, 11.
  Dam of Smuggler's Daughter,   Sire of Lady Thorne, 2:18¼; and 5
  2:24¾, and Abbott.   others; 23 sires of 92; 17 dams of
                                     24; all trotters.

3d dam, Dam of a great producer . . by IMP. ENVOY.

Description.— Here is one of good size, fine, and well gaited. He is broken double and single. Mollie D. is dam of Smuggler's Daughter, 2:24¾; and Abbott.

No. 122. STILETTO.

B. c., foaled May 13, 1891.

Bred by H. S. Russell.

BY

EDGEMARK (4), 7432, 2:16.

(To be trained and raced in 1893. Get in before the boom.)

Dam, MARY ARNOLD . . . . . . by ARNOLD, 966.
  (Inbred Abdallah.)   Sire of 3 and a speed getter, son of
                                     Abdallah, 164.

2d dam, LADY MONROE, 2:20¼ . . . by JIM MONROE, 835.

> Sire of eight; 2 speed getters; 10 producers; son of Alexander's Abdallah, 15.

Description.— This colt is small but very fast. He has been broken double and single, and trotted a quarter last year in 42 seconds.

No. 123. SMUGGLER GIRL.

Dam of Amurath, 2:28.

B. m., foaled 1881.

Bred by W. H. Wilson, Cynthiana, Ky.

BY

SMUGGLER, 927, 2:15¼.

Champion of the world in his day; sire of 9 from 2:19¼, 10 speed getters, and 9 producers.

Dam, MADAM POWELL . . . . . by BAY CHIEF.
Dam of Monroe Chief, 2:18¼.   Speed-getting son of Mambrino Chief, 11.

2d dam . . . . by TORONTO.
     Son of St. Lawrence.

Description.— This producing mare stands 15¾ hands and is sound and kind. She is the dam of Amurath, 2:28, at four years on a half-mile track. She was sired by Edgemark, Feb. 27, 1893.

No. 124. THEKLA.

(Out of the dam of Porcellian, 2:29.)

B. f., foaled January 1, 1892.

Bred by H. S. Russell.

BY

EDGEMARK (4), 7432, 2:16.

(Champion and unbeaten colt in his day.)

Dam, ILKA . . . . by SMUGGLER, 927, 2:15¼.
Record, 2:32½; trial, 2:24, 1881.   0 in list from 2:19¼; 10 speed getters; 9 producers.

2d dam, KITTY CHILDERS . . . . by TROTTING CHILDERS.
3d dam, KITTY . . . . by WOODBURY MORGAN.

Description.— Thekla is fair sized. She is mixed gaited. She has been broken double and single. Ilka is dam of Porcellian, 2:29.

No. 125.   RABBI.

Bay colt, foaled June 11, 1890.

Bred by H. E. Russell.

BY

EDGEMARK (4), 7432, 2:16.

(Champion colt of his age when made.)

Dam, RENA SIMMONS . . . . . by SIMMONS, 2744; 2:28.
   Sister to Col. Simmons, 2:22¾.   Sire of 20 in the list; leads all
                           Wilkes horses of his age.

2d dam, LENA. . . . . by CLARK CHIEF, Jr.
   Dam of one in 2:22¾.   Sire of a producer.

3d dam, ALICE . . . . by DOWNING'S BAY MESSENGER.

4th dam, FANNY . . . . by SWISS BOY.

5th dam . . . . by TAZEWELL.

6th dam . . . . by BERTRAND.

Description.—This colt is of fair size and is fast. He is broken double and single. Rena Simmons is full sister to Col. Simmons, 2:22¾. Rabbi trotted quarters in 40 seconds last year.

No. 126.   ROMA.

B. f., foaled April 27, 1890.

Bred by H. S. Russell.

BY

EDGEMARK (4), 7432, 2:16.

(Son of Victor Von Bismarck; dam by Edgewater.)

Dam LAURA WILSON . . . . . . by SMUGGLER, 927, 2:15¼.
   Dam of Kate Hamilton, 2:30.   Sire of 9 from 2:19½; 10 sires of 14;
                         and 9 dams of 10 trotters.

2d dam, BECK . . . . by WHITE OAK.
                         Son of Vermont Black Hawk, by
                         Woodford's Valentine, son of Red-
                         mond's Valentine, by Imp. Valen-
                         tine.

Description.— This colt is large and fast and is broken double and single. Laura Wilson is dam of Kate Hamilton, 2:30. Roma won forfeit as a yearling in a match at New England Breeders' Meeting.

92

No. 127. STANDARD.

B. c., foaled June 4, 1891.

Bred by H. S. Russell.

BY

EDGEMARK (4), 7432, 2:16.

(Will start in his class this year.)

Dam, MISS LONGFELLOW . . . . by LONG TAW.
Son of Longfellow.

2d dam, IVY H. . . . . by KINNET.

3d dam, AUGUSTA . . . . by AINDERLY.

4th dam, PRINCESS . . . . . . by IMP. LEVIATHAN.

Description.— This one is of fair size and is broken double and single. He is very promising.

No. 128. THISTLE.

B. f., foaled April 21, 1892.

Bred by H. S. Russell.

BY

EDGEMARK (4), 7432, 2:16.

(Entered in this season's stallion stakes.)

Dam, SONORA . . . . by HAMLIN'S ALMONT, 1829, 2:26.
Son of 23 from 2:12¾; 3 speed getters; dams of 12 with 5 in 2:20.

2d dam, SATEENE . . . . by MAMBRINO KING, 1279.
Sire of 26 from 2:10½; 7 in 2:20· 5 speed getters; 6 dams of 9.

3d dam, MIRANDA . . . . by MAMBRINO PATCHEN, 58.
Sire of 22; 39 sires of 100; 65 dams of 82.

Description.— This colt is fair sized and broken double and single. He is most promising and his breeding is ultra royal. Here ought to be a world beater.

No. 129.   SUCCESS.

Bay filly, foaled 1891; bred by H. S. Russell.

BY

EDGEMARK (4), 7432, 2:16.

(Champion and unbeaten colt trotter.)

Dam, GURGLE . . . . by POCAHONTAS BOY, 1790.
    Record 2:20.   Sire of 13 from 2:12½; 5 speed get-
                               ters, and 6 dams of 8.

2d dam, MATLOCK . .   . by GREY DIOMED.
    Dam of Gurgle, 2:20.   Sire of dam of Gurgle, 2:20.

3d dam . . . . by TOM HAL.

Description.—This is full sister to the preceding entry, and ought to make
a very fast mare. She shows for herself. She is entered in the Nutmeg $20,000
stake to be trotted at Charter Oak Park in 1894.

No. 130.   TEMPLAR.

B. c., foaled March 22, 1892; bred by H. S. Russell.

BY

EDGEMARK (4), 7432, 2:16.

By Victor Von Bismarck; dam by Edgewater.

Dam, ADDIE H. . . . . by ASHLAND CHIEF, 751.
    Dam of Whitefoot, 2:22¾, out of a   Sire of Black Cloud, 2:17¼, etc.; a
    great producer.   speed getter, and 12 dams of 13.

2d dam, OLD LADY . . . . by CAPT. WALKER.
    Dam of Charley Friel, 2:16¼; little   Sire of Molly Walker, dam of 3 from
    Miss, 2:20¼; Jessie Kirke, dam   2:13½; Old Lady, dam of 2, etc.; 1
    of Majolica, 2:15.   speed getter, and 7 speed getters
                             and producers.

3d dam, OLD LADY'S DAM . . . . by BROWN PILOT.

Description.—This is a royally bred fellow, and ought to be a race horse.
He will have a chance to show his ability, for he is entered in the Terre Haute
stake in 1894.

N. B.   Ransom is entered on $15,000 purse to be trotted at Hartford in 1894.   Stiletto, Success,
and Standard are in the Nutmeg $20,000 purse at Charter Oak Park in 1894.   Thistle, Templar,
Tallyho, Turenne, are in Terre Haute purse to be trotted in 1894.   All Colonel Russell's foals of
1892 are in the Charter Oak $20,000 Nutmeg purse to be trotted in 1895, and also in stake 47 of New
England Breeders.   Success, Sunbeam, Standard, and Stiletto are in stake 35 of New England
Breeders, to be trotted in 1894.

Consignment of G. H. Newell.

No. 131. **BEAUPORT.**

Bay colt, foaled May 10, 1890.

Bred by Dr. G. H. Newell.

BY

EDGEMARK (4), 7432, 2:16.

(Unbeaten colt of his age in his day.)

Dam, BLANCHE . . . . by LANDER'S KNOX.
Son of General Knox.

2d dam, LADY BLANCHE . . . . by LORD NELSON.
Son of Morgan Bellfounder.

3d dam. . . . . by IMP. WELLINGTON.

Description.— Bay colt, two white feet and a small star and strip. He is full of life but with a splendid disposition. He has only been handled by his owner and never for speed, but is fairly broken to harness. His dam was a 16 hand, 1075 pound mare, and showed quarters in 35 seconds. If anyone wants a roadster here he is, and the owner will sell him under contract to castrate him and return him safe to the buyer, if desired.

Consignment of Valley Stock Farm.

No. 132. **DOLLY.**

Black mare, foaled 1887.

15½ hands high.

BY

DESPOT, 4221, 2:29; (P) 2:24½.

Sire of Edward B., 2:24½; son of Dictator; dam, Spray, by Brunson; Son of Geo. M. Patchen.

Dam, dam of Dolly . . . . by HINSDALE HORSE, 826.
(Out of a great producer.) Sire of 5 in the list; 1 speed getter; dam of Malacca.

2d dam, DOLL WICKS . . . . . . by YOUNG NORTH BRITAIN.
Dam of Deck Wright, 2:19¼; N. J.
Fuller, 2:24; Black Ira, 2:30½;
grandam of Deck Wright.

Description.— This handsome black mare is broken single and double and is very intelligent. She is safe for anyone to drive. She produced a colt in 1891 which is a fair sample of her capabilities in that line. She missed in 1892 and was driven on the road, proving a first-class roadster, and can strike a 2:40 clip so easily that it is almost a surety, that with handling, she can beat 2:30. She is bred for a campaigner for her dam is out of the producer of Deck Wright and others. Despot is a son of Dictator with a trotting and pacing record. If any horse were to be retained in this lot Dolly is the one.

No. 133. **SNOW FLIER.**

Seal brown gelding, foaled 1887.

15 hands 3½ inches high.

BY

JEFFERSON PRINCE, 6212.

Sire of 8 from 2:19¼; 2 speed-getting sons; and the dams of Belmont Prince, 2:17¼, etc.

Dam, dam of Hazel Kirke, 2:29¼.   by PHIL SHERIDAN, 630, 2:26½.
Sire of Phyllis, 2:15½; and 10 others;
4 speed getters; 6 dams of 7.

Description.—This horse could beat any horse in Adams, N. Y., last winter, except Belmont Prince, 2:17¼. He is a sure 2:20 trotter and in any first-class man's hands can easily go there. He is a first-class road horse and can fly on any kind of footing. He is cheap at any price.

No. 134. **MAMIE C.**

Chestnut mare, foaled 1886.

Bred by Wm. C. Owens, Adams, N. Y.

BY

JEFFERSON PRINCE, 6212.

Sire of 8 from 2:19¼; 2 speed-getting sons and the dams of 2 race horses.

Dam . . . . by BACON'S ETHAN ALLEN, 356.
Sire of 5; 1 speed getter; and the
dams of 9.

Description.— This mare stands 15 hands 2½ inches and is well broken to single and double harness. She is a grand road mare and has shown a 3-minute gait when heavy with foal. She is a regular producer and will make anyone a great roadster and brood-mare. The seller has a colt out of her by St. Bel that will make a producer of his dam.

No. 135. **TOPSEY.**

Dam of Dick, 2:26¼ in 5th heat of a race; owned by Valley Farm.

BY

ETHAN ALLEN, 356.

Sire of 5; 1 speed getter, and the dams of 9.

Dam, grandam of Dick . . . . . . by RICH'S HAMBLETONIAN.

Description.—This mare is already a producer, and will be in the great brood-mare list before winter. She is a regular producer, and all her colts are speedy, level headed, and game. She has a two-year-old in the sale that will do to go to the races with.

96

No. 136.   SULWOOD PRINCE.

Bay colt, foaled 1891; bred by Valley Farm.

BY

SULWOOD, 6913.

Son of Sultan, 1513; dam, Lady Graves, by Nutwood, 600.

Dam, MAMIE C. . . . . by JEFFERSON PRINCE, 6212.
                               Sire of 8 from 2:10¼; 2 speed getters;
                               dams of 2.

2d dam . . . . by BACON'S ETHAN ALLEN, 350.
                               Sire of 5; 1 speed getter; dams of 9.

Description.— This will make a 16 hand stallion, and ought to be a great stock horse. He is fine, large, and can show better than a three-minute gait. He is well broken. He carries similar bloodlines to Kremlin, Stamboul, and Sunol, all noted for the production of extreme speed. This is one of the finest gaited colts on earth.

No. 137.   RICHESSE.

Full sister to Dick, 2:26¼; bay filly, foaled 1891; bred by Valley Farm.

BY

MAJOR BENTON, 9109.

Sire of Gov. Benton, 2:22¼, and Dick, 2:26¼.

Dam, TOPSEY . . . . by ETHAN ALLEN, 356.
     Dam of Dick, 2:26¼ .   Sire of 5; 1 speed getter; dams of 9.

2d dam . . . . by RICH'S HAMBLETONIAN.

Description.— Here is a fine bay filly; good sized, well broken in single and double harness. If this filly is not a star then there is no use in anticipating any good ones. For the amount of work she has had she is a wonder, for though not broken before January last she can now show a 2:50 gait. She has been driven double with No. 138, and it took a good horse to head them on the road.

No. 138.   ALBERT HAYNES.

Bay gelding, foaled 1891.

(Mate to No. 137.)

BY

MAJOR BENTON, 9109.

(Sire of Gov. Benton, 2:22¼; and Dick, 2:26¼.)

Dam, DOLLY . . . . by DESPOT, 4221, 2:24½.
                               Sire of one in 2:24½ ; son of Dictator;
                               dam of son of Geo. M. Patchen.

2d dam, dam of Dolly . . . . . . by HINSDALE HORSE.
                                         Sire of 5 in the list; one speed getter;
                                         dam of Malacca.

3d dam, DOLL WICKS . . . . . . by YOUNG NORTH BRITAIN.
    Dam of Deck Wright, 2:19¼; N. J.
    Fuller, 2:24; Black Ira, 2:30½.

Description.— Here is a trotting bred trotter and can prove it by his performance. He and Richesse can show a 2:50 gait double or either can do it single. He is a handy fellow and if ever he makes a break he will get back to his gait quicker than any other two-year-old. This is another Deck Wright in every way and when one looks up the heats he won in 2:30 or better, no one need ask for a better one.

No. 139.   ALLEN LASS.

Chestnut filly, foaled 1892.

Bred at Valley Farm.

BY

PRINCE ALLEN, 10114, 2:32¼.

(Separately timed in a race in 2:24½.)

Dam, a producer . . . . by BONNIE SCOTLAND.
    Dam of Hugo H., 2:25; Little Hugo
    (4), 2:30 trial.

Description.— This racing bred filly is unbroken, but will show speed to halter and is in every way a high-class article.

No. 140.   TOURISTE.

Brown filly, foaled 1892.

Bred at Valley Farm.

BY

SNOW FLIER.

(Son of Jefferson Prince, 6212; dam, the dam of Hazel Kirke, by Phil Sheridan.

Dam . . . . by MIDDLETOWN, Jr., 6056, 2:27¼.
    Full sister to Nelly Bly, 2:23¼;   Sire of Nelly Bly, Sylvia, and
    and Silvie, 2:27.   Blanche.

2d dam, BLACK KATE . . . . . by ANDREW JACKSON, 363.
    Dam of Nelly Bly, 2:23¼; Silvie,   Sire of Elmore Everett; 2 speed
    2:27; Mark B., 2:28; Black Bon-   getters; dams of 5 in list.
    ner, sire of A. G., 2:26; and
    R. C., 2:28.

Description.— This filly is not broken, but is a trotter by right of inheritance, for her sire and dam are both trotters and all out of producing mares. She will show for herself.

Consignment of A. B. Huron, Adams, N. Y.

No. 141. LADY HURON.

Bay mare, 16 hands, foaled 1885; due to foal in June.

BY

JEFFERSON PRINCE, 6212.

Sire of 8 from 2:10¼; 2 speed getters, and the dams of Belmont Prince, 2:17¼, etc.

Dam . . . . by IRA ALLEN.
Son of Ethan Allen, 356.

2d dam . . . . by TIPPOO HORSE.

Description.— This mare has produced three colts by Alcone, son of Alcyone. Her first foal was sold as a three-year-old for $1,200, her second I expect to put in the list this year, and her next, now two years old, is very promising. Her last is the yearling by Alcantara Prince, and she is due to drop another to the same horse in June.

No. 142. HURON BELLE.

Bay filly, foaled 1892. See No. 141.

BY

ALCANTARA PRINCE, 12210.

Son of Alcantara, 729, 2:23; dam, Souvenir, by Administrator, 357.

Dam, LADY HURON . . . . . . by JEFFERSON PRINCE, 6212.
Sire of 8 from 2:19¼: 2 speed getters; dams of 2 from 2:17¼.

2d dam . . . . by IRA ALLEN.
Son of Ethan Allen, 356.

3d dam . . . . by TIPPOO HORSE.

Description.— This is a fine, straight filly, and should, by her breeding, be oil in the can. She will show for herself at the sale.

Consignment of John Cheney.

No. 143. **JUNE.**

Chestnut filly, foaled 1891; John Cheney.

BY

ALPATRA, 15245.

Son of Alcyone, 2:27, by Geo. Wilkes; dam, Cleopatra, by Abdallah Prince.

Dam, LAURA M, 2:32 . . . . . . by GOODWIN'S CHAMPION.
Dam of Col. Kipp, 2:24¼.   Sire of 16 trotters, 1 speed getter;
                                                         3 dams of speed.

Description.—This mare is of good size, very handsome, and is broken double and single. She is good gaited, and could show 2:50 gait on the ice past winters. She will make a fast mare, and will trot in 2:30 this season with proper training. She is out of a producing dam, and her sire is out of a producing dam, and he will be given a record this season. He could trot in 2:25 last season. June is faster to pole; will show speed on day of sale. She is standard.

No. 144. **SOLTAIRE.**

Bay colt, foaled 1891; John Cheney.

BY

ALPATRA, 15245.

Son of Alcyone, 2:27; dam, Cleopatra, by Abdallah Prince.

Dam, MABLE C. . . . . by ARISTOS, 771, 2:27¾.
                                                    Sire of 14; 5 speed-getters; 3 dams of
                                                    speed.

2d dam, TWILIGHT, 2:27. . . . . by WASHINGTON JACKSON, 690.
                                                       Sire of Twilight, 2:27.

Description.—This is a large, nice bay, hind ankles white; broken double and single; good gaited and very attractive in harness. She has shown quarters in forty-two seconds as a yearling; will make a fast horse. She is very level headed, and comes from a family of trotters. She will go into the 2:30 list this season if given an opportunity. She is standard.

No. 145. MABEL C.

See No. 144. Bay mare, foaled 1882; Geo. W. Kingsley, N. Y.

BY

ARISTOS, 2:27¾.

Son of Daniel Lambert; sire of H. B. Winship, 2:20¼; 2:06 with running mate.

Dam, TWILIGHT, 2:27 . . . . . . by WASHINGTON JACKSON.
A game and speedy mare . . . . Sire of a race mare.

Description.— Mabel C. is broken double, single, and to saddle. She is safe for a lady to drive. She is large, good gaited, and fast, and showed a half in 1:16 as a three-year-old. She will beat 2:30 now if put in condition; is level headed and a good actor; will make a grand brood-mare and fast road horse. She can pull a wagon in 2:40 or better. She is standard registered.

No. 146, JESSIE W.

Bay filly 15 hands, 3 inches, foaled 1889.

Bred by Graham & Conley.

BY

DON CARLOS, 2097, 2:23.

(See front of catalogue, Briar Hill stallions.)

Dam, LIZZIE SMITH . . . . . . by SCOTT'S THOMAS, 919; 2:21.
Dam of Carldron, 2:22¼. Sire of 3; dams of 3.

2d dam, FANNY HOWARD . . . . by WOFUL.
Dam of Largusse, 2:25. Sire of a race mare and a producer.

Description. — This mare is broken double and single. She is nice looking and can show fast. She is out of a producing dam; should make a fast mare. She has been handled very little for speed; if worked this season should beat 2:30. She will make a grand brood-mare or fast road or track mare. She is standard.

Consignment of H. D. Kendall.

No. 147. **WILKES REGENT.**

(Standard.)

Chestnut colt, foaled June, 1892.

Bred by H. D. Kendall.

BY

ALLECTUS.

Son of Alcantara, dam Iola, (dam of Irene, 2:23¼), by Administrator. 2d dam, Jessie Pepper, by Mambrino Chief.

Dam, CAMILLA . . . by MELBOURNE KING.
Son of Mambrino King.

2d dam, HATTIE . . . . by FRANK ALLISON, 2:28.

3d dam
Daughter of Henry Black Hawk.

Description. — Chestnut colt. Strip in face, both hind ankles white; medium size, handsome, and nicely gaited. The great Prince Regent, 2:16½, was by Mambrino King out of an Alcantara mare, whose second dam was the famous Jessie Pepper. Here is a youngster, sired by one of the best sons of Alcantara, with a producing dam, and Jessie Pepper for his second dam, out of a mare by one of Mambrino King's best sons. Wilkes and Mambrino Patchen blood through Mambrino King and Alma Mater, with Edwin Forrest and Morgan crosses, represent a rare prospect in the trotting horse and this colt will prove a prize.

No. 148. **CAMILLA.**

(Standard and registered.)

Bay mare, foaled 1886.

Bred by Harry Townsend, New Glasgow, N. S.

BY

MELBOURNE KING, 1962.

Son of Mambrino King, 1269; dam, Helen McGregor (dam of Almont Rattler), by Rattler, 501; g. d., by Brignoli, 77; 3d dam, by Pilot, Jr., 12; 4th dam, by Grey Eagle, thoroughbred.

Dam, HATTIE . . . . by FRANK ALLISON, 4218. Record, 2:28.
Son of Blackbird, 4217; dam, Lucy Pope by Harris' Morgan.

2d dam . . . .
Daughter of Henry Black Hawk.

Description. — Bay mare, 15½ hands, strip in face, one hind and one fore ankle white. Sound, broken, single and double; kind in disposition and safe for a lady to drive. Low-gaited, wears no boots, and gives every promise of speed.

Her blood lines are worthy the most careful attention. The splendid per- formances of the progeny of her grandsire, Mambrino King, are too well known to require extended mention. Mambrino King, "the handsomest horse in the world," son of Mambrino Patchen, the greatest brood-mare sire, and grandson of Edwin Forrest, grandsire of Nancy Hanks, has no better son than Melbourne King, sire of Camilla. To the blood of his sire he adds the Black Hawk-Morgan strain through Rattler, sire of his dam. Brignoli, sire of his second dam, has seven producing daughters and is a son of old Mambrino Chief; his dam by thorough- bred Woodford, sire of the dam of Woodford Mambrino and Wedgewood. Back of this is the inestimable Pilot, Jr., cross, and the stout four-mile blood at Grey Eagle. With this rich heritage from her sire, Camilla combines the best Morgan and Long Island Black Hawk blood. Melbourne King's get are trotting fast and several will doubtless enter the list this year. Camilla produced last June a promising colt which is also entered in this sale. She certainly will prove very valuable either as a brood-mare or a trotter.

Consignment of J. A. Ripley.

No. 149.   MAGGIE McIVOR.

Bay mare, foaled in 1884.

BY

ALCANTARA (4), 729, 2:23.

Sire of 51 from 2:12½; 12 speed getters; dams of 7 from 2:14¾.

Son of George Wilkes; dam, Alma Mater.

Dam . . . . by GREEN'S HAMBLETONIAN, 158.
Sire of Nelly and of the dam of Green Boy; full brother to Volun- teer, 55; sire of 31 from 2:11¼; 30 sons with 98; 41 dams of 45.

Description.—Maggie McIvor is a very handsome bay mare, 15¼ hands high, weight 1,000 pounds. She is perfectly sound and can trot very fast. She is a mare of great resolution and an ambitious roadster, but perfectly safe for a woman to drive. Mares by Alcantara are proving great brood-mares and have produced Prince Regent, 2:16¼; Ægon, 2:18¼; Diable (3), 2:14¾; Princess Royal (2), 2:20; Ovid (3), 2:15½, etc. Maggie McIvor should make a great brood- mare. She had one foal in 1891, which is said to be very promising.

www.ingramcontent.com/pod-product-compliance
Lightning Source LLC
Chambersburg PA
CBHW032155010726
47493CB00008BA/2704